I0728580

Red Beans and Rice with Cornbread

By J. Lew

Copyright © 2017 by J. Lew

Red Beans and Rice with Cornbread
By J. Lew

Printed in the United States of America

ISBN 9781946806161

All rights reserved solely by the author. No part of this book may be reproduced or transmitted in any form or by any means without written permission from the author.

www.jlew-books.com

Dedication

To my dad (U.S. Air Force, Korean War), my father-in-law (U.S. Navy, WWII), my brother (U.S. Army, Vietnam War), my wife's brother (U.S. Marine Corps), and my brothers, brothers-in-law, sister, and daughter (U.S Air Force, U.S. Army, and U.S. Navy), not including myself (U.S. Air Force); and to all our fellow brothers and sisters in arms who served before us, with us, and are currently serving — may the Lord watch over you as He watched over us while you travel in harm's way.

It really is a family affair when a band of brothers and sisters join together and bond as one unit with a common goal. No one can ever tell why God brings us together, but friendship and camaraderie cause some of our best and worst memories.

Table of Contents

Introduction

Thursday, July 17, 1969 – The Replacements

Corporal Drummon walks out of HQ to find Sergeants Rawls and Williams. Colonel Weathersby is waiting on replacements and wants Rawls and Williams to get them up to speed ASAP. The base has been under fire every night and he's losing men on every attack. Drummon walks past a couple of the solders, stops, turns around and then asks, "Hey guys. Have you seen Staff Sergeant Rawls and Sergeant Williams?"

"Last time I saw, they were over in the mess tent," one of the soldiers informs him.

He thanks him and keeps walking until he gets to the mess tent. He finds the two of them sitting on the wooden sidewalk outside the tent complaining about the food. "Hey Sergeants."

"What's up?" they ask at the same time.

"The CO wants you guys to welcome the new troops when they arrive."

"When are they due in?" Rawls asks.

"In a few minutes."

"Yeah, yeah, we got it," Williams replies, removing his cap to rub his head before dumping his food on the ground.

Drummon walks away, while Rawls looks up at the tree line waiting for the chopper to break into view.

"I'm too old for this." Rawls complains.

"If I remember right, you said the same thing last year." Williams reminds him.

"It's not getting any easier out here; the bush seems to get thicker every month. I swear! The last time we went on patrol the trees were shooting at me. It's bad enough having the VC shoot at us from their tunnels, but when the trees you are hiding behind start shooting at you, it's time to pack your bags. When that happens, there ain't nowhere to hide."

"I'm a big fan of napalm myself. It helps us with those shooting trees and thick bush you're talking about." Williams leaning back on his hands.

"Yeah, I hear that. And I also hear those choppers, so let's go and introduce the cherries to the bush." Rawls says.

Watching the Hueys land, they both stand a ways off from the helo pad wondering what Uncle Sam has sent them this time. After the Hueys lift off, the replacements wander off the pad, some of them looking lost while others walk a little gung ho. The new troops look as if they want to ask where they should go to be briefed. A private points in the direction of Rawls and Williams. Nine new cherries walk up to the sergeants as they lean against a pole just below the pad. "Okay gentlemen," Williams starts.

"Hold on, Sergeant!" Corporal Manson shouts while dropping his gear to the ground. "You mean to tell me you watched us get off the pad while you were just leaning against this pole without escorting us to our bunks?" He looks at Sergeant Rawls and asks, "Where can I find the CO? I'm not one of these privates this boy can command..."

"Shut your trap, Corporal! You speak when you're spoken to." Williams shouts.

"Actually Sergeant," he goes on, looking at his nametag. "Sergeant Williams, I was talking to Staff Sergeant Rawls here. Don't you have some shoes you should be shining somewhere?"

"Ohhhh!" shout the other privates, laughing.

Sergeant Rawls pulls a coin from his pocket and flips it.

"Heads!" shouts Rawls.

"Tails it is," Williams says with a smile. "I'll see you later."

"It's been a long flight, boys. Just point me to my bunk," Corporal Manson nervously demands.

"Follow me, funny guy, and the rest of you too. I have somebody you'll want to meet."

They follow him, anxiously wondering if they should have laughed at Manson's remark to Sergeant Williams. They walk up a hill to just a few feet from the unit's outhouses.

"Gentlemen, I want to introduce you to the crappers."

"Oh, hell no!" Corporal Manson shouts. "I didn't come all this way to clean no damn shitters!"

"Shut your piehole, numbnuts. All of you, get your gear and lay it down over there by those logs. Move your asses!" he shouts. Eight of the replacements run to the logs and lay their gear down, waiting to see what happens next.

"Hell no!" Manson refuses, walking in circles with his hands on his hips.

Sergeant Rawls is in Manson's face. "I don't know what rock you crawled out from under, Manson, but out here you do what you're told." Turning around, he calls out, "Corporal Gaines! Bring me my shotgun." Corporal Gaines runs up to Rawls and hands him his shotgun. Rawls pumps the shotgun and points it at Manson. "You have three seconds to move your ass."

Reluctantly, Manson turns and walks over to the logs with the others, muttering under his breath.

"Get these boys some gloves and instruct them on the art of shit burning," he orders Gaines.

Gaines gets the gloves and hands them out to all the cherries. Not wanting Manson to snatch the gloves from his hand, he drops Manson's at his feet.

"Now I don't know what you jackasses did to piss the old sergeant off, but I want you to know that you picked the wrong guy. He's been here since '67, and trust me, you don't live that long in this jungle being stupid. Take a look at the man next to you."

They all look at each other.

"Now, take a look at Manson."

They all look at Manson.

"He'll be the first in this group to go home in a body bag. Everything you do out here you learn from it!" Corporal Gains shouts.

"Sorry Corporal, but I can't see what I'm going to learn from cleaning these outhouses," Private Stevens complains.

"Over there you have gasoline and diesel fuel," Gains says, pointing, "and on the back side of the crapper, you have a door. Open the door and you will find cans cut from fifty-gallon drums. You drag those cans out about thirty feet from the crapper. Over there next to that mortar hole, you have empty cans, which you'll use to replace the cans you removed. Take the full cans and pour diesel fuel and gasoline in each one, and then you get one of those stir sticks and you stir the soup while it burns. I hope you understand, because I don't plan on repeating myself. Gentlemen...."

He points to the crappers as he walks away and takes a seat next to Sergeant Rawls.

Stevens and Wayne walk over to the crapper in the center, cautiously opening the flap door to look at the can full of crap before dropping the trap back down. Manson hurries to the one on the end and lifts the door while holding his breath, pulling the can out about four feet before letting it go. Not being able to move out of the way, he gets splashed with about a gallon of crap and then vomits.

"Out here if you're in a hurry, you can trip one of Charlie's booby traps, or step on one of his punji sticks. That's lesson number one. You learning anything, Private Stevens?" Corporal Gains shouts.

"I'm learning!" Stevens shouts.

The rest of the guys grab cans of their own, pulling them slowly while trying not to splash any crap on themselves. The day has been really long and all they want is to get a shower and find some food and their bunks. Sergeant Williams walks up right when they are finishing.

"As I was about to say before I was so rudely interrupted, out here you listen to those who've been here for a while, and you'll have a good chance of going home when your tour is over. The nine of you will be assigned to either Sergeant Rawls or myself. Over the next week, you'll be briefed on surviving this rock — that is, unless Charlie decides to teach you himself. Ain't nothing any of us can do about sniper fire or mortars being fired on us by Mr. Invisible out there, but if you listen and keep your fool head down it's possible you'll live. When you're on patrol, make sure your canteens are full or empty; Charlie has good hearing. Don't be so inclined to watch the ground; Charlie likes to attach spikes in tree branches about head or chest high.

Keep watch at all times. Listen and learn, people. That's how you leave here walking."

"Hey Sarge, we know where the crapper is, so where's the shower?" Stevens asks.

"Not much of a shower, but you'll find one on the other side of the camp. In back of the camp, some engineers built a small building for us. You'll have to fill the cans above your head with water, so use it sparely because ain't nobody toting water for you girls out here."

"Sounds good to me," says Stevens.

"Okay… Stevens, Wayne, Trenton, Levette, and Manson, follow Sergeant Rawls. And the rest of you, follow me. We'll show you where you'll bunk."

"One hell of a way to start," Wayne whispers to Stevens.

"From now on, we keep our mouths closed. This will be something I'll tell my kids someday, but not something I'm writing home about."

"You and me both, I'm going to wash this day off me, and put it behind me."

Chapter 1
Where Do We Go From Here

After hanging up the phone, I think about what she said that stunned me: *This is just a room that needs to be cleaned and aired out.*

"I'll call Ben Truman," I told her. Truman is an exterminator and handyman that I have used for years to maintain the office and the grounds. I figure I'll explain to him what I need and ask if he can please hurry.

I stare out of my office window worrying about the future of this business. Now, I'm anticipating my appointment that is just a few hours away and wondering if I should cancel. What an incredible morning Marie must be having at this time. I really wish I could do more.

I think of all the time that has flown by. It's been twenty-nine years since I started this business, and I can't say I'd change a thing — I just wish my Jimmy were here to take over for me. Sighing and sinking into the chair while rubbing my face, I think to myself, *Retiring is a dish best served when you can afford it, but money isn't an issue. So why am I struggling with it? The Lord has blessed my family and me, and it's time to start a new chapter in life. And besides I'm getting too old for all this.*

I whisper to myself, "Going to bed has gotten a lot easier while getting up in the morning has gotten a little more complicated." Dropping my arms into my lap, I stare up at the ceiling for thirty minutes just thinking. *When your giddy-up requires a plan in steps, you know it's time to pass the baton to the next generation.* The business is doing very well with all the construction going on here in Texas and in three of the bordering states. In the reflection of the window, Brandon Daniels walks past the office door.

"Brandon!" I call out. I turn around in my chair, and Brandon takes a few steps back and sticks his head in the doorway.

"Yes, Jim?" he answers.

"I have an appointment in a few hours, and I want you to take my calls while I'm out. I'm waiting on Wilkins Construction to call back. They're building a small bridge in Texhoma on the Oklahoma side. They want to rent a few column forms for a job they are pouring next week, and the same for J & J Construction. They were asking if we have the forms they need for a job site near Willington. I just emailed you the information, and I want you to give Chuck a call down at the yard and make sure we have the forms. If we don't have the forms, call Donald at Formco and see if they have what we're short, and if so we can rent what we need from them.

"Okay, is there anything else?"

"Yes, get back with Marie at J & J to let her know we have the forms and send them a quote with a ten percent discount."

"Sure thing," Brandon replies. "Will you be back today, seeing it's Friday?"

"I'm not sure yet, but that's why I want you to handle those two accounts for me today."

"Alright, I can do that. Is there anything else?"

"No, taking care of those two will be enough, but get ahold of Chuck ASAP. I don't want to lose J & J's account."

"Okay, I'll give him a call as soon as I get back to my desk."

"You do that, and thank you."

"You're welcome." Brandon walks away.

Swinging the chair around, I can't help but stare out the window at the one thing that connects me to my son Jimmy. I also think about the day I decided to bring Brandon into the business. Scratching my arms, I get lost in thought. Bringing Brandon onboard was a long-shot fourteen years ago — that boy and his brother were nothing but trouble. I told Sam, my brother-in-law, that I would give him a chance, but the first time he got picked up by the law I would not hesitate to fire him. Sam said he understood and thanked me for taking him on. He wanted me to bring on both his boys, but that was a losing proposition.

And as it turned out, all Brandon needed was a little kick in the butt, a bit of guidance, and someone to be stern and not accept his excuses. Turned out he was a real hustler and a go-getter. It's too bad I can't say the same for his brother Mack. Being firm only made him more rebellious. When that boy wasn't late for work, he didn't come in at all. There were times when he only showed up on payday and argued that we were family and family don't short-change family. That was a chapter well worth closing. Marie encouraged me to get Brandon more involved in the day-to-day operations of the business and to allow him to do more to help the company grow. It turns out that promoting Brandon to VP of Sales after Marie's retirement five years ago was the right decision. There are times when others can see what I can't and I have to trust their judgment.

Marie knew that if she retired, it would force me to get Brandon more involved in the business.

The phone rings, and Janet, the company's receptionist, answers. It's a new customer calling the office while Jacob is handling an account and Brandon is busy with my accounts. Janet calls me and asks if I can take the call. Then, after an hour of exchanging information with the customer, I let him know that Brandon will manage their company's account, and I thank him for choosing our company for their business needs. I walk out of the office and stop by Janet's desk.

"I'm going on a walk," I say. "I'll be back before my noon appointment."

"Alright," Janet replies. "I'll see you when you return."

I start walking down the sidewalk and watch others pass and greet one another.

"Hello!" says a pedestrian. I return the greeting and keep walking.

I know that I should call her, but knowing her, she will just announce that she's okay. I should let her finish her work, which is a nice way of saying I'm bothering her or I'm in her way even though it would be a phone call.

"Why now? Why did she go and open that door today?" I ask myself, staring up at the sun. "Is she still trying to force my hand into retirement?"

As usual my thoughts run away with me. In a low voice, I walk down the trail and murmur, "Poor girl, she's going through it all by herself. I guess she's right, though — I should go ahead and let her know that I'm ready to call it quits." I wipe the sweat from my face and gulp down some water. "Oh Jimmy, you inspired so many things. I just wish you were here with your mother and me to enjoy them." Then I walk the two-mile trail and come back through the door.

"You guys miss me?" I ask.

"Oh yes, terribly," says Brandon. "That's why we are all standing here waiting for your return."

Mockingly, I add, "I take it the copier is on the fritz again?"

"Yes, it is," Jacob replies. "How'd you know?"

"It's the only time the two of you have an excuse to be up here trying to impress Janet. I've always figured it takes two of you to determine if one of you should call to have it serviced."

"Really," Jacob replies.

"Well, Mr. Stevens, you know how I love it when these handsome men speak copier talk… like the do-hickie turns the what-cha-ma-call-it, and the thing-a-ma-bobber is causing the thing-a-ma-jig to jam."

"Oh, thanks Janet," Jacob whines. "Hey Brandon, what's the number of that bus that just ran you over?"

"Oh, just me?" Brandon retorts.

Now, Jacob is striking some of his bodybuilding poses and says, "And here I am working out all hard at the gym getting all pumped up. To think I wore one of my tight Polo shirts today!"

Janet is fanning now and wooing him as he walks back to his office. I laugh and grab another bottle of water from the break room fridge, and then tell Brandon and Janet, "I had a body like you guys once. Then Marie spoiled it and woke me up."

The office is full of laughter. Janet grabs my attention as I walk into my office.

"I think it's time to retire this old copier and get a new one," she says. "With all the money we spend on maintenance we could have purchased a new one."

Without turning around, I stop at the door and think about how much maintenance it takes just to keep me going.

With a smirk, I reply, "I think you are right, Janet. Why don't you look up a couple of copiers and compare them? Then, when you find a good replacement, you can buy it."

"Oh, I'm going to miss you guys so much," Janet says.

"Yeah, right," Brandon replies.

"Here comes the bus!" Jacob shouts from his office.

"Really, I will… all that testosterone what-cha-ma-call-it stuff," she says in a gruff voice. Janet leans back in her chair while Brandon flexes his chest muscles and walks away.

"Bam!" shouts Jacob "That's the 918 bus."

Sitting back at my desk, drinking water and resting after my walk and waiting for the time to pass, I look up at the clock. It's been three hours since Marie called, and now it's ten minutes until eleven.

"Well, I guess I'd better go and get there a little early." I walk out of the office and stop at the door, turning the lights off, not wanting to look back as I close the door behind me.

"Are you on your way to your appointment, Mr. Stevens?" Janet asks.

"Yes, all my calls will be directed to Brandon's office, and he'll call me if there's anything urgent."

"Will we see you after your appointment?" she asks.

"No, I have a feeling Marie has other plans. You guys have a good weekend."

Everyone in the office thanks me and bids me to do the same. Smiling, I see Janet watching me as I walk out of the office and down the hall to the front door, and step out into the parking lot.

I stand at the door of Jimmy's 1970 Pontiac Bonneville Convertible I purchased over thirty years earlier. A year ago, I had it fully restored like new and only drove it on the days of my appointments. Placing my hand on the roof of the car, I close my eyes for a moment and reminisce about the days before and after I bought the car for Jimmy.

Marie and I were anxiously awaiting the return of Corporal James Evert Stevens II from his first tour in Vietnam in December 1970. James volunteered to join the Army; he and his best friend Günter Wayne went to the recruiter's office together in late 1967, when they were nineteen, and enlisted. I could not convince him to stay at home and go to college. His response was always the same.

"I can attend college after I get back."

They figured a lot of guys their age were volunteering for service.

It was in June of 1970 when President Richard Nixon said the Vietnam War was coming to an end as a result of the plan they had instituted. Nixon stated in a conference that the United States would be following a new program called "Vietnamization." Joyfully, Marie was excited to hear the news, as were many others across the nation. Monday night, she complained about the water running in the toilet. I decided to take the next day off work to fix the toilet that ran all night and annoyed Marie until I got out of bed and turned the water off at the wall. Then, on Tuesday December 8, 1970, Marie and I were just finishing up a late lunch. I was walking back to my chair to watch more coverage of the war with a glass of milk and a slice of pound cake, and Marie was washing up the last of the dishes when there was a knock at the door. A Casualty

Notification Officer and a chaplain waited for someone to open it. I set my milk and cake on the end table next to my chair and answered the door. My heart fell into my stomach, and I knew immediately at that point that James would not be coming home for Christmas. With my eyes closed, I braced myself and stood against the wall, shaking my head. I took in a deep breath and covered my eyes with my hands for a brief moment before Marie came out of the kitchen and asked, "Who is it at the door?" When she saw my expression and the two men in uniform standing in the open doorway, she fainted.

With a sigh, I take the keys from my pocket, unlock the car, climb in, and close the door. I sit there with my eyes closed, gripping the steering wheel and thinking back thirty years.

I remember opening the garage and just staring down at the car, thinking of how I could not bring myself to sell it or even get rid of it — it was the one thing that gave Jimmy hope. Oh, how he was looking forward to coming home to drive his new car.

The 1970 Chevy Bonneville has a wood-grained sport steering wheel, A/C, cruise control, a power seat and windows, a 370hp 455 engine, and an 8-track tape player installed. The interior is large and plush with soft seats and wood-grain accents. After sitting under a tarp in the garage for nearly thirty years, I decided to take it off the blocks, put new tires on, and see what it would take to restore the car back to factory condition. I had only ever driven it from the dealership home, and when we knew Jimmy would never drive it, I backed it up into the garage, put it on blocks, took the wheels off, and locked it up for the next twenty-nine years.

I open my eyes, turn the key, and the car roars to life like it has just been taken off the showroom floor. I stare at my office from the car — the office is dark, but I can see the clock on the wall and some of the old pictures of days long forgotten. *Will Brandon take them down and replace them with his own?* I wonder.

"Why am I trying to cleave to all this?" I ask. "Marie has been trying to get me to turn this loose for five years now, and now that she is making changes at home, I know she will really push for my retirement. Maybe next month I'll make the announcement; maybe I'll do it next week. That will really make her day."

I put the car in reverse and back out of my reserved spot. Driving out of the parking lot, I pass some of the buildings that have changed over the past thirty years. I can still remember what the area used to look like; having all the pictures in my office is a great reminder, of course. Many of the changes seem to make the things of old fade away, for not many of the things in those days can be seen today. Pulling onto the highway, I push the accelerator and feel the power the old girl still has. The ride is smooth and handles great as it moves down the highway at sixty-eight miles per hour. I smile as I cruise in the Bonneville, wishing I had dropped the top and driven it as a convertible. I drive for ten minutes on the highway and get off on the feeder road, and then turn onto a stretch of old road that has gone through changes in all the passing years. I drive for about five minutes on the old road, and then into the parking lot to find a place to park.

Chapter 2
The Drive to Anywhere

Alice's restaurant has gone through several changes as of late, but it's the place to go for the best comfort food in town. If you do not know how to get there, you'll pass it by and then stop and ask for directions; that is, unless you're that guy who once drove from Topeka, Kansas to Nome, Alaska on a single tank of gas and never had to ask for directions once.

The restaurant has been in Alice's family for more than seventy years. They couldn't increase the size of the parking lot because there was no property close by that they could purchase. It looks as if they've had a facelift done in the last month or so since my last visit. Alice is retired and now her grandson Anthony runs the restaurant. After her husband passed away six years ago, things began to drop off a bit and the care of the restaurant started going by the wayside.

Anthony moved to Warm River after he graduated from Le Cordon Bleu Culinary School, a year before her husband Andrew took ill, and started working as a manager of the restaurant. After the death of Alice's husband, Anthony started managing it for her, and then recruited trustworthy people and began to pick up around the old place. Alice is a small black woman who greets and cares for all her guests; she treats everyone as an extension of her family. The first time Marie and I visited the restaurant was when we decided to take a drive just to get out of the house. We both fell into a deep depression after the burial of our son, and neither of us found the strength or desire to leave the house. Every night I would hold the letter that notified us of Jimmy's death in my hands; it was opened but I did not read it. With the television off, I would stare into the darkness with tears in my eyes and try to figure out whether Jimmy's death was instant or if he suffered for a while. I remember waking up early in the morning and finding that I had spent the night sleeping in the chair with the letter in my hand before it fell to the floor by my feet. It was like déjà vu each morning — a nightmare impossible to shake. I would sit in that chair after musing around the house and stare at the Christmas tree, the lights of which would never be lit. *Christmas is coming,* I would think, *and Jimmy will never again be here to celebrate it with us.* Why him? Why couldn't it be me? Why did he have to die so young? Why? And why didn't he listen to me and go to college? One question after another went through my mind, but there were no answers to be found.

One morning the phone rang, and I finally had the strength to answer it; it had been more than a week since either Marie or myself had answered the phone or the door.

I picked up the phone. "Hello."

"Well, good morning Jim." It was my manager calling, checking up on Marie and me. "We were getting a little worried — I'm calling to see if there is anything I can do to help."

"No," I responded. "We're just trying to get through this and make sense of it all."

"Well, I can respect that. You know, you have our support; and if you need more time just keep in touch and let me know."

"Thanks, Richard. I'll do that," I agreed.

"Oh, and Jim?"

"Yes, Richard?"

"I dropped by and saw there were many flowers and cards at your door from well-wishers. You may want to bring them in; it gives the wrong impression that no one is home."

"Thanks, Richard," I said. "I'll do that. Anyway I'll probably be back at work after next week; I have to get motivated, and getting back to work will help me do that."

"Take your time, Jim. We're here for the two of you if and when you need us," Richard said.

"Thanks again, Richard. Goodbye."

"Take care, Jim. See you when you come in."

I heard the phone ring and the well-wishers at the door, but I just wanted them to go away. And yet, now that I'd answered the phone, it gave me a bit of encouragement. I stepped outside the house for the first time in over a week. Neither of us had ventured outside since the funeral. When I opened the door, some of the flowers and cards fell inside, and I could see letters and cards with flowers from members of the family, and a few from the neighbors. I was overwhelmed with emotions and fell to my knees, crying at the door. I looked out into the driveway and saw the car I had purchased for Jimmy. Still crying, I wiped away the tears and stood on the porch, taking in long breaths.

I walked out into the brisk air and leaned against the car, weeping more as I thought of Jimmy. I took another deep breath and looked out into the streets. In the window of my neighbors' home I could see a small service banner hanging there, showing that they had a family member serving in the war. I noticed some kids braving the cold weather, not unlike me, as a couple of cars drove by and blew their horn and waved. Walking back up to the door of the house, looking at my empty window, I realized that I'd never hung a banner for Jimmy's service in the Army, but of course everyone knew that he was serving in Vietnam.

I walked up to the porch to clean up all the flowers, cards, and letters that were lying around the door. At that point Ann, Marie's sister, drove up and parked at the curb in front of the house. I was still in my robe and slippers and wasn't sure whether I wanted to entertain company, but thought, *At least she's family*. I invited her in and she gave me a big hug and said she knew sooner or later that I would either answer the phone or open the door.

"I've come by every day and was getting a little worried about the two of you," she said. "Is Marie up?"

"She hasn't been up in a week, and I don't know what to say to her to help her out of bed."

"Well," she said. "You have to first get yourself together before you try helping someone else. It's a little hard to motivate someone when you are in the same boat."

"I'm doing my best," I said.

"What you need to do is find a place to go, or just drive and let the miles help put the past behind you. God has a way of getting you through these trying times, you know," Ann said wisely.

I shrugged my shoulders at her suggestion.

"I'll tell you what — you can go back out there in that cold air in your robe and slippers, and I promise it will put you in the hospital. And what will that do for Marie?"

"Not much, I suppose."

"Then you need start seeing things a little clearer, sit down, and think things through," Ann went on.

And then she talked to Marie and stayed by her side for the rest of the day, only leaving to give me a chance to clean myself up and help motivate Marie to do the same. Another week went by and Marie was up and walking about the house while I returned to work. I began to wonder whether a change in occupation was in order and wasn't sure if I wanted to continue in the architecture business. I began to put a plan together for starting my own business. Over the next three weeks, Ann and I tried to get Marie to leave the house, but without any success.

One cold Saturday morning in January, I woke up to an empty bed. After fussing about in the bedroom and then around the living room, I noticed that Marie wasn't in the house. So I put on the pants I'd worn to work two days before and tightened up the belt on my robe and walked out of the house into the backyard. The garage has a guestroom attached, and Jimmy was allowed to make it his own bedroom after his fourteenth birthday. It's a single room with a small closet, a toilet, and a sink. It has a small gas-burning heater in the wall about five feet from the floor and a small air conditioning unit that hangs through the wall to the porch. When Jimmy wanted to bathe, he had to come to the house. The room has a small porch attached where Jimmy would sit on one end of the porch and bounce his rubber ball off the door of the storage room on the other end. The door to his room was closed, but I could see the light was on. When I reached the door, I turned the knob, but could not enter because Marie had locked it from the inside.

"Go away!" she shouted.

I didn't want to leave her alone out there, so I stood at the door for a little while until it got too cold and couldn't stand there any longer. I walked back inside the house and watched her from the kitchen window.

Inside, Marie was preparing to clean our son's room. Sitting on the bed, she took all of Jimmy's clothes and folded them, placing them neatly in each drawer. After that, she went to the closet and removed the few clothes he'd left hanging; she folded them and put them in a drawer as well. All of his personal childhood belongings, she tucked in the corner of the closet. On his dresser sat a couple of trophies, his brush, his rubber ball, and his baseball glove against the mirror. She dusted the top of the dresser and wiped the mirror clean. From the mirror, she saw his bike against the wall and started to cry. From the house I could only see her shadow as she walked past the window of Jimmy's room that looked out into the backyard. The other window faced the driveway that led into the garage.

There were many times when Jimmy was in his room, and I would drive up and Jimmy would knock on the wall three times and I would respond with three knocks from inside the garage. When I walked past the window, we would wave at each other. Now with Marie in the room, all I could do was wait until she was finished, and hope it would help her move on. At about noon, while I was watching TV, she walked into the house and went straight to the bedroom without speaking. I turned the TV off and walked into the bedroom and asked, "How are you?"

"Fine," she said quickly.

"Do you need help with anything in Jimmy's room?" I asked.

She stared at me for a few awkward seconds.

"I am finished and the door is locked," she snapped.

"Okay," I said, turning around and walking back to the living room. At that point I turned the TV on and pretended I was watching it. It was very slow at first, but I decided that it was time for that ride to anywhere and hoped it would be good for the both of us. I put the letter from the Casualty Notification Officer in my top dresser drawer, never to be opened again. Reluctantly, Marie put herself together for what she was hoping would be a very short ride.

Mildly, she protested, "I'm really not up for this right now."

I strongly urged her to go with me. I remembered a campsite we'd visited when Jimmy was twelve years old and thought we would journey in that direction. I believed taking the long route to get there would be best. I didn't tell Marie where we were going, but we both went quietly to the car, climbed in, and just started driving. We headed east on Highway 86 and then southeast on Highway 287 until we reached Highway 83 North to make the drive as long as possible. I hoped it would give Marie time to overcome her loss.

I wanted her to talk to me, so I tried a little small talk to get her to say something.

"Do you want to stop and get something to eat?" I asked.

Marie shook her head and said, "No." She kept looking out her window. After nearly two and a half hours, she asked, "Where are we going?"

I looked at her and said, "Just driving right now, unless you want to go somewhere specific?"

"Well, hell, James," she said angrily. "Why don't we just keep driving until we run out of gas?"

Laughing, I said, "Like when we ran out of gas off Route 66 when we were dating?"

She sat silent for a few seconds and then said, "Oh no, your car didn't run out of gas and neither did you!"

"You mean, neither did we," I replied.

She laughed a little at the thought and said softly, "We were so much younger then, and more flexible too."

We both laughed for a little while until she slowly came out of her shell and kept up the small talk until we reached Canadian, a small town in North Texas just shy of the Oklahoma border. We stopped there and got a bite to eat, and after watching a few trucks and cars towing boats, Marie asked, "Isn't this the town we were at when James was younger?"

"Yes, it is," I replied.

Then she suggested, "Since we're this close we might as well go to that lake where we camped when we brought James out here for our trip."

I was happy she suggested it.

"Lake Marvin," I said.

"Yes, that's it," she replied.

"It's less than fifteen miles east of here, so we should make it there in less than twenty minutes," I said happily.

Eagerly, I paid for lunch and hurried back to the car. We stopped by a service station and told the attendant to fill the car with Ethyl. Then I paid the attendant and we headed toward the lake.

"We haven't been here in more than eight years," I mentioned.

Marie looked at me and said, "We'll stay only for a little while and then head back home, okay?"

"Sure," I said, "whatever you want."

Arriving at the lake, we found it a bit cold but peaceful. Wrapping herself tighter in her coat, Marie hugged me as we walked around the park. Stopping at the edge of the lake, we stood there and she began to cry, wiping away the cold tears as she asked, "Do you remember the first fish he caught?"

I laugh and say, "Oh my, I believe it fit in the palm of his hand, and he wanted you to cook it for him?"

"Yes!" she exclaimed. "He would not take no for an answer, would he? When I had him clean it, there wasn't much left to cook, if I remember right. He used that pocket knife you bought him to clean it and then I fried that poor little thing extra hard trying to burn it so he wouldn't want it."

"Yes, but that didn't help at all; he ate it anyway."

We both laugh.

Everywhere we walk it brings back fun memories of the weekend we had camping here. We held each other as we walked around the lake for a while, talking about the times we all had together. Before long, it was getting late in the evening and the sun was setting a little low in the sky.

"Well, we'd better get started back home. It's getting late." We both sighed as I hugged her a little tighter.

"Jim," she called.

"Yes?"

"Thank you," she said, and then kissed me.

On the drive home, I thought it would be better to take the short route by heading straight down Highway 60 South to Highway 87 South. We found the warmth of the car comforting because neither of us knew how cold it was until we got back into the car with the heater blowing on high.

As we drove, we noticed that most of the restaurants had closed, and we were getting pretty hungry.

"I sure hope we can find somewhere to eat," I said. "Otherwise we'll have to eat moldy bread and meat."

She looked at me and laughed. "Umm, nothing spreads better on a sandwich than a little mold," she joked.

"I believe we can top that with a little wet mold on the bologna to help it to spread a bit easier," I added.

Talking, laughing, and making jokes were good for passing the time, but our stomachs were growling, letting us know we had to find something soon.

Two hours into the drive, just ahead on the left, we could see lights coming from an old restaurant neither of us had noticed before. When I pulled into the parking lot we debated whether to get out of the car or just drive away.

"Well," Marie said aloud. "It's this or moldy sandwiches." We looked at each other and then decided to get out. Walking to the door, and pulling on the handle, we found it locked; our hearts fell and our spirits dropped when we pulled on the door and couldn't get in. We had already turned back to the car when a lady's voice called out to us.

"Hello there," she said.

We turned to face a small black woman with her hands in her apron pockets.

"We're sorry," said Marie. "We thought the restaurant was still open."

"We just closed and locked the door, but you look a little tired and hungry," said the woman. "Come on in."

Marie and I apologized and walked back to the door. "We wish that we had gotten here a little earlier."

"You just come on in out of the cold air. We only have a little bit of red beans and rice with cornbread left, and if you two like that, you are welcome to it." The woman paused and introduced herself as we stepped in. "My name is Alice," she said.

Introducing Marie and myself, I replied, "This is my wife Marie, and my name is Jim."

"Well, come on in, Jim and Marie," Alice said warmly.

Both of us were hungry, and Marie and I graciously stepped inside and sat at a table near the window. Alice stepped behind the counter and walked back to the kitchen where her sister Maggie was getting the mop and bucket ready. She took two plates off the shelf and laid a bed of rice down, and then poured a cup of beans on top.

"Girl, you acting just like Mama — you don't know how to turn people down," Maggie groaned. "That door was closed and locked and should have stayed that way until morning."

"Hush, and give me a couple of spoons out of that drawer there," whispered Alice.

"I'll get them for you," Millie said as she reached into the drawer. "Why do you always have to complain?"

"Why are you in my business?" Maggie replied.

Millie handed Alice the spoons with one hand, and staring at Maggie, she placed her other hand on her hip. "I'll help you with the water," she said, looking back at Maggie who was shaking the mop handle at Millie.

"Millie!" Alice called. "Cut me two pieces of cornbread and put them on a saucer."

"Sure girl," Millie replied.

While we waited on our food, Marie asked, "Have you ever noticed this restaurant before?"

Looking out the window, I tried to see where exactly we were.

"I can't say that I have," I replied. "Maybe I just breezed by it before, but I'm not sure."

"Do you know where we are?" Marie asked.

Still looking into the darkness out the window, I said, "As much as I hate to admit it, I'm not sure."

"Oh my Lord — the Lord must be returning when a man admits he's lost!"

"Now hold on, I just said I wasn't sure. I know what highway we're on, but I don't know what part we're at."

Laughing, Marie asked, "You want me to ask for directions?"

Pushing her gently with my shoulder, I said, "Don't worry, Marie. I'm as dependable as a homing pigeon."

Still laughing, she said, "Well, stop pecking at the window, Mr. Homing Pigeon."

"I know where we are," I said reassuringly.

"Sure dear, but they're bringing our food now. You might want to lose that lost look on your face."

"When we leave here," I said, "I'll take us right to our drive, you'll see."

"I know you will, dear. Just remember to turn right out of the parking lot. Or will that be a left out of the parking lot?"

"I should give you a snaky lick in the ear when we get back in the car for that."

"Oh, please don't," she protested with a laugh.

Alice and her sister Millie brought out our food and two tall glasses of water, and left us to eat.

"If you need a little more, I'll get it for you," Alice said.

"Thank you." I blessed the food, and Marie and I began to eat.

"I don't know if I'm just hungry or what, but this is really good," Marie said, smacking her lips. "There is sausage and ground beef in the beans, with onions and I think celery. The spices are wonderful, the rice is cooked to perfection, and the cornbread is moist — a little sweet, but it really tastes great."

"What did you say, honey? Your lips were smacking so loud between words I couldn't hear or understand anything you said."

She hit me with her spoon and laughed, wiping away her tears.

"I can't remember the last time we had so much fun," Marie cried.

We ate two helpings and were ready for a long night's sleep. At that point, we looked up to get Alice's attention, and saw she was just finishing up mopping the floor behind us. She stepped behind the counter and washed her hands before walking over to the table.

"We apologize for taking so long here, but the food was wonderful. Can we have the bill now, please?"

Alice refused to accept any pay.

"Come back again," she said. "You can pay for your next meal."

Marie tried protesting, but Alice would not accept our money. After our efforts failed, she walked Marie and me to the door.

Speaking to Marie, Alice said, "I saw you crying at the table. Is everything alright?"

"It's going to get better," Marie replied.

"It seems as though the two of you may be going through something, and I'm sure everything will be okay soon."

Marie hugged her and said, "Our son was killed in Vietnam and this is the first time we've left the house in six weeks."

Alice slipped her hands into her apron pockets and clutched the letters she carried with her every day.

"Well, you look like good Christian people," she said. "Would you mind if we pray?"

They prayed in the cold night air, and when she had finished, she assured them that she knew God would help them through it all. Then Alice said good night and told them to be careful on their way home.

Chapter 3
Alice's Hugs

I smile as I reminisce of that cold night so long ago. We frequented the restaurant at least once a month after that, always the last ones in and the last ones to leave, but never staying past the closing hours.

Looking at my watch, I notice that Alice's restaurant parking lot is now half full. I hope Marie won't have any problems finding a place to park when she arrives.

I climb out of the car, locking it with the key. Just as I lock it, I hear the chirping of those who use the remote for their cars. I pat the car on the roof and say, "Things have changed a lot, haven't they, old girl?" Then I turn toward the door; and when I am about to open it, a young lady walks out, so I gesture for her to step outside. But before she can come through the door, two young people rush in and rudely pass as if there are no seats left in the restaurant. She shrugs her shoulders and thanks me before I walk in. Alice greets me with a hug and asks, "How are you faring today?"

"Oh, I'm doing fine today," I reply. "Arthritis was a little slow on the draw this morning, so I'm hoping to stay ahead of it as the day passes."

She laughs. "Keep at it, and you and arthritis are going to have some long conversations first thing in the morning. It might be slow today, but tomorrow it gets another chance."

We laugh and I pat her on the shoulder and ask, "So how have you been? I didn't see you the last time we were here; I missed my hug."

She tells me, "Well, being retired has its advantages and disadvantages; I can't come in like I used to. I let my grandson run everything now so I just come by every once in a while. Usually when I'm bored sitting at home watching the traffic go by. Every now and then, I go on the road with my granddaughters and see a little bit of the country. Last month, we were in the mountains of Arkansas." Holding her hand over her heart, she lets out a sigh. "Just beautiful out there."

"I bet it is." I say.

Alice changes the subject. "Speaking of retirement, when are you going to retire? It's a lot less stressful."

"Marie wants me to make that announcement as soon as five years ago. I wasn't sure at first, but I think I'm ready now."

"Good for you," says Alice. She grabs my arm and adds, "You take that beautiful woman and go out and see how beautiful this country is. I bet she'll just fall in love with it."

We talk for a while, and then she walks me to a booth at the window and lets me know that someone will be by when I'm ready to order. I thank her. "I hope to see you here the next time we come by — I don't know how I'd feel about walking in and not getting our hug."

"Oh, you'll be okay," she says, waving her hand at me.

I sit down in the booth next to the window and wait anxiously for Marie to drive up. I find myself getting lost in thought, and then notice the man staring back at me has gone through some changes. A plumper face and grayer hair, to start, and a little wider at the shoulders and hips. I hold my left fist under my chin and pull my shirt tight against my biceps with my other hand, and then flex and see that there is barely a change in the bump that used to be a muscle. Earlier in the office, I noticed Brandon and Jacob's young toned bodies with the biceps and chests of bodybuilders.

I never really had a chest like that, and I never had the arms of a bodybuilder. I'm not skinny, but not fat either. I guess I could have gone to the gym a couple of times a week, but work has always consumed me — at least, that's what I have been telling myself. "Oh well," I whisper. "You're stuck with what you have, old boy."

A silver Infinity drives up and takes the attention away from my thoughts. A young couple gets out smiling and carrying on a cheerful conversation. I watch as they walk across the small parking lot to the front door of the restaurant, and then my attention is drawn to a Ford pickup truck with an extra-long bed as it drives through the parking lot looking for a good spot, only to find a tight space next to a small car at the end of the drive.

While waiting on Marie, I want to know how my wife's morning went. Based on my conversation with Ben after he left the house, I have a pretty good Idea of how it went. *Well, if the old girl can open that door, I guess I can retire and stop trying to work through my memories of Jimmy.*

I look over at the classic I drove in and watch as others pull up, get out of their cars, and walk over to the Bonneville to admire its mint condition. Still waiting, I look up at Alice as she greets her customers at the door; things have changed a bit since our first fateful visit thirty years ago. The restaurant has a larger sign, a fresh coat of paint, new flooring, a new menu, and the small table we sat at has been replaced with this booth. I'm sitting in the same spot looking through the same window as that night; Marie joked with me for putting my hands against the window, cupping my face trying to figure out where we were. The menu has changed over the years, but there is one thing that Alice and her family have been feeding their customers since 1932, and that's red beans and rice with cornbread; her grandson Anthony promised that he will keep that on the menu.

Chapter 4
The Last Letter

December 5, 1970

Hello Mom and Dad,
It's really late and sleep is a luxury these days. Every day we are thankful for another morning. We got a group of new guys in today as replacements; man, they are really young. I talked to this one guy from Philly and he said that he was seventeen years old. I'm afraid to make friends with any of them because I may be the one pulling their dog tags later. I really miss you guys. I'm a short-timer now and I only have eleven days and I'll be sporting my new Bonneville, sweeeeeeet. This letter won't be long, the NVA (that means the North Vietnamese Army) has picked up the attacks on the camp so I'll just say I love you two and I'll see you when I get back.

Love you,
Jimmy

Jimmy addresses this letter to his mom and dad, and then folds it and places it in the envelope and licks the seal closed. He kisses the envelope and...

"Stevens," Sergeant Woods calls from outside.

"Yo! What's up?" he answers.

"Put that letter away and get your ass out here. Keep quiet and stay low; we need you on the mortar with Rev."

Jimmy cuts off the flashlight he was using to write his letter and quietly leaves his bunker. He gets down in the pit with Reverend Sergeant Leo Daniels; Rev is a minister from Florida who got transferred in from the 25th Infantry Division.

"What do we have out there, Sarge? I can't see anything."

"You've been in the light too long. Close your eyes for a few seconds and then open them slowly and look at the edge of the woodline. All kinds of movement. This is it, baby; they got us boxed in like Custer's last stand. Pay close attention here; we're going to lay down a line of fire to the northwest of the camp and then redirect just north of our position. You've been through this a few times now, so I expect you to take control just in case I don't make it. We have a lot of cherries here and they need someone like you to lead them."

"Don't talk like that, Sarge," Stevens says.

"Don't tell me how to talk, Stevens," says Sarge. "You just do what I tell you. Besides, I got a bad feeling about this."

"You can count on me, Sarge. Who's in what hole?"

"Wrong way is over there to our left on the fitty. Goodtime and Ramos are set up in the hole just to our right, and in the front of us with a couple of grease guns is Private Dancer. When I tell you to keep them mortar rounds coming, I mean double-time it. If it gets too hot we'll drop a couple rounds and then advance to the rear through the wire on Route 66."

"You got colorful words for retreat, Sarge. What was that? Advance to the rear?"

"Yeah. That means haul ass, boy, and don't get yourself shot."

Jimmy closes his eyes again and covers them with his hands. He counts to ten slowly, opens his eyes, and scans the treeline.

"Hey Sarge, you have those green eyes on you?"

"Yes, why?"

"Give them to me quick." He looks through the starlight scope and sees a group of VC flanking them on the far left of the camp. "You might want to take a look to our left flank." He points to the left, almost to the rear of their position.

Sergeant Daniels jumps on the radio to call the commo bunker for a line adjustment.

"VC massing on our left flank, I repeat, VC massing on our left flank, we need to un-ass immediately."

"Roger that," came the voice on the other end of the line. "Good eye, Sergeant."

"Not me. That was Stevens."

"We'll try to strengthen that side of the camp; we have foo gas and guys with clackers in the area, so do not readjust your target at this time. I repeat, do not readjust."

"Roger that," he acknowledges. "You have to be a dinky dau to be out in this man's jungle. I don't know why the hell we have to wait until they fire. This waiting is for the birds — hell, we can see them, so let's be the first to throw the punch."

An enemy mortar round blasted one of the foxholes they set up earlier for mortars, so they decide later that night to change the placement to the position they are in now.

"Damn Sarge, that would have been us," Steven whispers.

"Shut the hell up and fill the tube, dammit."

They launch a few rounds on the enemy's position to the northwest and then focus their fire on the position just north of their foxhole. About five minutes into the battle, they are running low on mortar shells in the pit, so Rev orders Stevens to get more from the dump.

"Hurry up and keep them coming," Sarge orders.

Just as Stevens turns for a second trip to run and get more shells, a mortar hits the pit and throws Stevens to the ground; his ears are ringing from the blast. He looks up in a daze and sees Sarge's boots from where he was last standing. He struggles to get up and then runs back to the front of the pit to push sandbags out of the way. He starts firing his M-16 and screams in the dark.

Someone yells, "The enemy has breached the perimeter. Fall back, everybody fall back."

He fires a couple more rounds and then starts running out of the pit to find Route 66 when another shell explodes to his right side, throwing him into a pile of sandbags that used to be a bunker. Unharmed but dazed, he turns and fires at four VC who are running through the camp firing at those in retreat. Then the thought comes to him: *Advance to the rear.* As he picks himself off the pile of sandbags and turns to get a start for the wire just ahead of him, he feels a prick in his side and then in his shoulder and falls to the ground. He looks up and a VC that is running toward him with his bayonet pointed in his direction; he lifts his rifle and fires a few shots to drop him. He struggles to change his clip and then pulls a couple of grenade pins and tosses them toward the running VC, and then empties his clip before a VC runs at him from the darkness and shoots him several times in the chest.

The call for Puff the Magic Dragon, an AC-47 gunship to fire on the camp, comes a couple of minutes too late for Corporal Stevens, Rev, and many others. The F-4 Phantoms fly in dropping napalm and five hundred pounders on the tree line and killing fields. After the gun ship makes an end to the VC's run on the camp, except for the groaning, all is quiet until morning. Then Captain Hodges and those who made it out of the camp return to inspect the damage.

"Weeks," Hodges calls, "Get a search party out for Colonel Weathersby and the Major."

"On it, sir," Sergeant Weeks acknowledges.

After a few minutes, Lieutenant Davies runs up to report.

"Captain," he calls out. "We found the Major buried under the commo bunker. And by the way, Colonel Andrews and a couple of platoons are outside the wire and coming in."

"Thanks. Lieutenant, keep the search going for the colonel," he calls out to Sergeant Weeks.

"Yes, sir?"

"Round up some men for cleanup," the captain orders.

"Already on it, Captain," replies Weeks.

Captain Hodges walks back to the wire where Colonel Andrews and his men are walking through and salutes.

"It looks like you men had one hell of a battle here," Colonel says.

"Yes, sir. This was the worst of all the attacks. Even worse than the one last month when they breached the perimeter; we were able to kick their butts back across the wire then, but this time we did the running."

"I can see that," the colonel replies as he scans the area.

"All the others were mere harassment when they tested the wire and our strength in the camp. This time they threw everything at us, even the kitchen sink."

"Well, take me to Colonel Weathersby, son. I need to brief him on what's going on."

"No can do, sir — I have a search party out now looking for him somewhere in all of this mess."

"Captain!" Lieutenant calls out. "We found him, and he's still alive. Doc Walters is patching him up, but he'll need to be medevaced out of here with the others."

"Where is he?" Hodges asks.

"Outside the wire, sir. He made it out, but I guess he was shot up so bad he was running in the wrong direction. That's why we couldn't find him in camp or among the rest of us."

"Did you call for a dustoff, Lieutenant?" asks Colonel Andrews.

"Yes, sir, the call went out immediately, sir," replies the lieutenant.

"Well, take us to him, Lieutenant." The Colonel commands.

"This way, sir." Acknowledges the Lieutenant.

"Captain Jacobs." Calls the Colonel.

"Yes, sir."

"Radio Command and let them know Colonel Weathersby is wounded and Major Franks is dead. Then get some of our boys to help look for more of the wounded."

"Yes, sir."

They run to where Colonel Weathersby fell, and where Doc has already patched him. Colonel Andrews kneels on one knee to speak to Colonel Weathersby while he lies on his back.

"The helicopter will be here soon to medevac you out of here. You'll be well taken care of, so you hold on now, you hear me? You still owe me a bottle of scotch, and I plan on collecting it," he says while scanning the area.

Captain Hodges kneels at the colonel's side.

"Right now we have everybody on the ground doing everything we can to help out. We have it all under control."

Colonel Weathersby simply looks up at him and tries to squeeze his hand in response.

"How soon will that helicopter be here, Lieutenant?" Captain Hodges asks.

"I think I can hear them now, sir."

Everybody looks up to see the helicopters just clearing the trees. Then Colonel Andrews looks down at Weathersby. "Your ride is here. Try not to give the nurses too much trouble, you hear?"

Colonel Andrews and Captain Hodges stand and move out of the way so the troops can carry Weathersby to the helicopter. They watch as he and the others are loaded onto the choppers streaming in, and then watch as they fly off.

Colonel Andrews orders more men to span out and look for others who may have gotten lost in the confusion.

"Captain," Colonel Andrews says, looking at him and scratching his head, "it seems you're the new CO until we can get someone in to relieve you."

"Yes, sir. It seems that way, sir."

"You'd better be up for the challenge because there seems to be more of this coming your way. We had a fire base set up to support you guys, but the VC must have had a better plan because they hit about four of our bases simultaneously."

"Well, at least now I know why they didn't answer our call for fire support."

Colonel Andrews holds his head down and kicks at the grass. "Well, they didn't fare too well either, but they must have had an enemy in the camp. In the first few minutes they rained down on the camp and were able to knock off a squad of howitzers and tanks, and then overrun the base. We flew in support gunships, but it was too late — nobody survived."

"I guess it was that way for all the camps, right?" asks Hodges.

"It was. Anyway, let's clear out one of the bunkers and make a new command center for you. Then I'll brief you on what Command expects of us out here."

"Yes, sir."

Two weeks after the bodies were sent back home, Goodtime finds a sealed and addressed envelope that Corporal Stevens left behind; he hands it to Sergeant Ramos. "Damn, where'd you find this?"

"One of the newbies found it behind Stevens's bunk on the floor. I guess it was the last letter he was writing to his folks back home."

"I'll get it to the CO and he'll make sure it gets on the next chopper out to Stevens's parents."

"Wasn't he due to go home?"

"Yeah... four days ago."

Chapter 5
A Step in the Right Direction

Marie can't believe that it's been over thirty years. She gets up earlier in the morning to prepare my breakfast before I leave for work, and then goes back to bed and stares up at the ceiling. She tries to go back to sleep, but sleep evades her. In all the years that have passed, it seems she has accomplished as much as she could, and now all she wants to do is enjoy life. Even though she has everything she wants, she still feels empty and wants desperately to put Jimmy's death behind her. She retired from her position as vice-president of the company five years ago. She wanted to do more than get up every morning and go to work.

"It's time to travel," she often tells me. "Even if it's just to spend the weekend at a bed and breakfast and relax, and forget about all the headaches of the business. It's time to pass the torch and move on."

Since her retirement, I've found more excuses to stay until I felt comfortable enough to pass the business on to our nephew Brandon.

"You have to let go," she tells me. "You have to let the next generation take over."

Sitting at the table with me before I leave for work, she says, "We have the money to live comfortably for the rest of our lives and beyond, if ever there was such a thing. You remember when Ann couldn't get Fred to let their children carry on the family business?"

"I do," I answer with a nod.

"Remember what a mess that was? It became too much for the both of them by the time they got to their late sixties, and then his health got so bad they were forced to give it up. By that time the company had gone into despair and none of their children ever got the training to take over the business. Eventually it failed after twenty years of success."

"You saying the same will happen to our business?" I ask.

"No, but I'm not sure if it was because none of their children were ever in the decision-making process or if they just got tired of trying to get new ideas past Fred, and they just let it fail because they did not care anymore."

I sit staring at my plate, and then walk away from the table to leave for work.

"Jim," calls Marie. I turn around. "I want you to really get Brandon trained up and let him take on the responsibilities so you won't have to worry about the business. It will continue long after you retire."

"I'll think about it," I say, and then kiss my wife and say goodbye.

Marie walks back to the bedroom and climbs into the bed, putting her arm across her eyes as she says to herself, "There are times when you just have to say goodbye and live the life you wish you could have lived when you were younger and too broke to pay attention."

Lying in bed, she thinks of the years that passed since her retirement and how difficult it's been to get me to retire. It's hard to fall asleep because her thoughts pass the time.

She thinks back to the time she fainted after seeing the two men in uniform at the door come to inform us that our son died after his small base camp was overrun by the enemy. She tries to put it all together, and thinks to herself, *I can only remember sitting in the chair with Jim holding a towel on my head and clutching my right hand and the chaplain holding my left hand. I screamed in protest and snatched my hand away from the chaplain. It was hard for me to accept them in our home, bringing news that they let my son die. I remember screaming at them and saying it was their fault before ordering them to leave.*

"Get out! Get out of my house," she'd shouted.

I don't remember Jim accepting the letter, or him walking them to the door as they apologized and offered their sympathy. After a couple of weeks, Jim and my sister Ann convinced me to get out of bed and try to eat and drink more for my health. Jim called the doctor because he was worried that my health was getting worse. Slowly, I recovered and began to get around the house, but I refused to leave. I remember the first week after the burial, I got up in the middle of the night looking for Jim, and I found him asleep in his chair with the letter of notice on the floor by his feet. I could see he was hurting just as much as I was, but I did not know how to comfort him because I was looking for comfort from him.

"Two sad souls with broken hearts were having a tough time trying to manage their way through a maze of sorrow," she whispers, reminiscing.

Even after I found the strength to get around the house, it was about all I could do and nothing more.

Marie sighs and looks over at the clock. She sees that it is already eight twenty-four, two hours since I left for work. Pulling herself up slowly out of the bed, she sits on the edge of the mattress and stares at the room, trying to get the day started. Sighing again, she stands and walks lazily to the vanity, where she looks into the mirror and then at a picture of us when we were in our twenties.

"Wow, we were really young then," she says, looking in the mirror at herself.

Reaching down and opening the drawer to her vanity, Marie closes her eyes and removes a box. She sets it on the vanity, opens her eyes, and pulls out the letters that Jimmy sent to them while he was in Vietnam, including the one that came to them after he was buried. She never opened that letter and never told me that it came in. Turning to look at the dresser, she stands and wonders if she should open the top drawer — where I left the Western Union letter from December 8, 1970. Reaching into the drawer and retrieving the letter, she finds another letter underneath. Another letter from Jimmy.

"What is this?" she wonders aloud. "I remember getting all the mail when it came in. When did this one come?"

Then she notices that it was addressed to James E. Stevens I at her mother's home address. She has never read the Western Union letter, not even when she saw it on the floor by my feet. Looking through my drawer for more letters, she finds only the one. Jimmy only used that address to write once. Marie cannot fathom why on earth I would hide it from her. Taking in a deep breath, she closes her eyes and says, "I think I'll opt to open the Western Union letter first."

EST Dec 8 70
GOVERNMENT PD WASHINGTON DC

Mr. AND MR. JAMES EVERT STEVENS I
3015 W. 15TH STREET
WARM RIVER, TEXAS

THE SECRETARY OF THE ARMY ASKED ME TO EXPRESS HIS DEEP REGRET THAT YOUR SON, CORPORAL JAMES EVERT STEVENS II, DIED IN VIETNAM ON 6 DECEMBER 1970, FROM WOUNDS RECEIVED WHILE IN COMBAT OPERATIONS WHEN HIT BY HOSTILE SMALL ARMS FIRE. PLEASE ACCEPT MY CONDOLENCES.

Her arms drop to her side. Folding the letter, she cries and walks back to the vanity. After a moment, wiping away the tears, she begins to open the letters she had read when they were sent home prior to his death. She hasn't opened these letters for over thirty years.

When I read them, I don't care what order they're in. I'll just open the first one I pull out of the stack.

June 14, 1970

Hello Mother and Dad,
I hope you're not worrying too much at home over me. I am doing fine here.
I wish I had some of your chicken and dumplings right now. I'm not going to tell you what I have been eating here because you would not approve. Let me just say the soup is missing a few ingredients.
It's a little late and I'm sleeping on my bunk (cot) with no mattress so it's as comfortable as it can be. I am getting enough sleep so if you see bags under my eyes in the picture that's the result of sleeping too much. Speaking of sleeping too much, I have to get a few winks before it's my time for guard duty.

I miss you guys,
Jimmy

April 18, 1970

Hello Mom and Dad,
You remember Gunter Wayne, don't you? Well, that guy is a fool. Last week we were on our way back from a patrol and I don't know what that fool ate, but the whole time he was complaining about his stomach hurting. We were less than a klick from base camp and he passed gas, and it was a mess. When we got to this slow-moving stream he decided to pull his pants down to wash his butt and pants as we waded through, and you would think we were walking in mud. Man, was Sergeant Rawls ever mad — we ran across that stream

as fast and as quiet as we could. When we got back to basecamp Rawls made Gunter go directly to the showers. When Gunter undressed and saw all the leeches covering his butt and unmentionables, he screamed and tore out of the shower stall like a racehorse out of the gate. Man, the whole camp laughed at that fool. Doc had him standing for ten minutes pulling those little bloodsuckers off of him. I would have taken pictures, but he was embarrassed enough already.

I got your letter dated March 25, 1970, a couple of weeks ago. We have been a little busy, so I'm only now getting the chance to write. I wish you could send some of that spaghetti and meatballs here, it really sounds good right now. Hey Dad, have you been down to the old fishing hole lately? Gunter's dad sent him a picture of a mess of catfish he caught there two weeks ago. When I get back, that is one of the things we are going to do.

I'll write more later.

Love you,
Jimmy

Looking down at the letter with only my name on it, Marie pulls the top open and slowly unfolds the letter.

November 6, 1970

Dear Dad,

I really don't know how to say this to you, but I'm really scared. We got notice that the North Vietnamese Army is really massing, and I'm not sure what to think. I don't think it will be the best of Thanksgivings this year. Gunter, Sergeant Williams, and a few newbies were shot and killed in a fire fight early this morning. For the first time, we had to fight the NVA from inside the camp. I thought we were going to have to retreat back to our escape route, which we call Route 66. We were nearly overrun, but we were able to fight them back with the help of the Air Force dropping bombs so close to the camp, we had to take cover at the bottom of the foxhole.

We've been harassed on a daily basis (that means they fire mortar shells at us two to three times a day or more). It only lasts a couple of minutes at a time. A lot of our guys were shot up pretty bad, and our numbers here are a lot smaller now, and I'm not sure if we will get reinforcements in time. The dead and wounded will be air-vac'd out in a little while. I'm writing you from my foxhole because we're not sure if they will try again. We are told we have to hold our position, but we are outnumbered at least ten to one. I'm so close to leaving here I can taste it. My hands are shaking as I write this letter. My tour will be over and I hope to be home next month on the 16th. I cried when Gunter was killed; he was my best friend and one of the best soldiers in the outfit. Sergeant Williams was a really *cool guy that looked out for Gunter and me; I really feel alone now.*

I guess this is why they tell us not to be in too big of a hurry to make friends; it hurts so badly when they get killed. I'm writing you this letter addressed to Granny Mae's so that Mom does not see it. Please, don't ever show her this letter. I'm really, really, really scared for the first time since I've been here. I have to tell somebody and I hope that you are not angry with me. I want you to know that I love you and respect you very much. I wish that I had something better to write.

Love you,
Jimmy

Covering her mouth while reading the letter, tears fall down her face.

"Oh my god!" she cries! "Oh… my hands are shaking right now. I never knew what my baby was going through, and now I wonder what is in the letter I have not opened."

Her tears soak the envelope that was addressed to Granny Mae's house and the old ink spreads across the paper. She throws it on the vanity and sits there staring at the unopened letter, wanting to open it and yet wanting to leave it sealed just as Jimmy's bedroom door had been locked for the last thirty years. Now angry and puzzled at what to do next, Marie knows that she wants to bring me the letter and ask me about it, although she knows I was just honoring Jimmy's request not to ever show her. Holding her head back and looking up at the ceiling, she puts her hands over her face and says, "Okay."

Sitting at the vanity for a little while staring at the picture of the two of us, Marie gets up off the stool and puts both letters back in my top drawer. She leaves them where I left them and closes the drawer. Then she stands with her back to the dresser, her eyes closed and her fist balled tight.

She says to herself, "Do it, Marie. Do it, just as you did thirty years ago. Just do it."

She opens her eyes, and then marches across the floor to the door. She opens it and marches through the kitchen to the back door before stopping in her tracks. She closes her eyes again and says, "Open the door and go out there."

She slowly walks out across the backyard and stands at the door of what Jimmy called his sanctuary. She unlocks it and stares at the room. She frowns, holding her hands to her nose for the stench.

She turns quickly shouting, "Oh my god!"

Filled with anger, she storms away from the door, turns around, and shouts again.

"Thirty damn years!" she screams. "Thirty years and I have not unlocked this damn door. And now just look at it — it's a mess."

She walks back to the door and takes a long look into the room as she holds her nose.

"Damnit," she says. "Those rats have been living in Jimmy's room and just left their musty odor behind."

She stomps toward the door wondering what to do next. She's afraid of all the spider webs so she refuses to enter. She reaches in and slams the door shut and storms back into the house.

Calling me crying, she says, "I opened the door to Jimmy's room and couldn't believe my eyes."

Over the phone I suggest we cancel our appointment. I say I'll come home and help her clean it up.

She tells me, "We will do no such thing. We have always kept our appointments, and this is just a room that needs to be cleaned and aired out."

There was silence at the other end of the line.

She asks, "Did you hear what I just said?"

"Yes, I heard," I reply. "I was just taken aback by your comment."

"If you want to help me, call an exterminator and have him get here as soon as possible. The rest..." She lowers her voice. "The rest, you leave to me."

"I'll do whatever you want me to do. I'll get ahold of Ben and have him come out. Is there anything else you need me to do?" I ask.

"Just be at the appointment," she says.

"Okay," I say, and then hang up the phone.

Marie dials her youngest sister Betty and asks her if she can come over and help clean Jimmy's room.

"You did say Jimmy's room, right?" Betty shouts.

"Yes, Jimmy's room." Marie replies.

"I'll be there right away," Betty says.

Marie then calls Ann to see how she is doing. And if she feels up to it, would she mind coming over to help clean Jimmy's room?

"I'll be there as soon as I get dressed," she says, hanging up without saying anything else.

"I'll call a maid service," Marie says to herself. "They could help me with all the rat droppings and other messes those nasty rodents left behind."

She goes back to her bedroom to get dressed in her cleaning clothes, and waits for everyone to show up. Her sisters arrive within thirty minutes and Ben shortly thereafter.

Marie opens the door for Ben and says, "The room has been locked for thirty years. I don't know where to tell you to start, so I'll leave that up to you."

Betty and Ann are looking over Ben's shoulder and holding their noses.

Ben asks, "Is it okay to open the windows before I get started?"

"Don't ask," says Marie. "Just do what you have to do to get the job done."

Then she turns and walks away with her sisters close behind her. Ben opens both windows in the room and goes about spraying and knocking all the spider webs from the walls; he realizes the job is bigger than he thought. The ladies wait on the front porch for him to finish. Both of Marie's sisters hug her tight and tell her how brave she is.

With tears in her eyes, she tells her sisters, "All these years I have been telling Jim to put that business behind him and move on. I know he has poured his life into that business as if it was Jimmy, and he has procrastinated for the last five years."

"Well," Ann says, "I know how that is. That hardheaded man I married only retired because of his health, and by that time, the kids were so fed up with the whole thing they just let the business fail."

"That's why I retired hoping Jim would do the same and that… didn't happen. I want him to retire and move on with his life, and yet I live in a house with a room that I have refused to enter for thirty years. And when I finally open the damn thing, I find it infested with generations of rats and spiders and God knows what else. How can I tell him to move on when I'm still holding on to the past?" Marie sighs loudly.

"You can't. No more then he can by holding on to that business," Ann says.

"Girls, I opened that door in hopes of finding it the same way it was the day I locked it on January 9, 1971, only to find it occupied by something else. I suppose this is a reminder that nothing lasts forever — and of how rodents can change your perspective on life in the single opening of a door." She sighs again. "It shows you how the Lord is so very patient with us. All these years, I've been on Jim and now I find that the Lord has been waiting on me to open that door. I'm mad! I'm very mad at this whole thing. I'm ready to go back there and knock that room down and the garage with it."

Betty asks, "What were you going to do if it was still in the same condition it was in thirty years ago?"

"Well, to be honest, I wanted to simply open the door and think of all the time that passed and clean it out so out-of-town guests could stay in it when we entertain them. Now I guess this mess has just changed everything."

Betty leans over her shoulder and pushes her and asks, "Do you think this will help you get through it better? I mean, maybe what you needed was a little kick in the rear end to get you over the wall."

"I don't know," Marie replies. "But everything did change when I opened that door, I tell you." She laughs. "Now I have to move on, and I hope to motivate my husband to do the same."

Ann looks at her and says, "I think you've beat that mule to death. You need to focus on Marie and let the Lord deal with Jim."

Marie meets her sister's gaze and asks, "Whose side are you on?"

"I have always been on both your sides. I'm just saying you should let him lock the door to his business so that he can see what you did when you unlocked that door. Telling him what you think he should do won't change a thing."

"Yeah girl," Betty interjects, "all that nagging just drives him right to what you are trying to get him to leave."

"Oh, thank you. I feel like I'm stuck between the Dear Betty and the Dear Ann columns of the newspaper. Why don't you two just shower me with your sarcasm?"

"Girl, you know we love you. We're always here to comfort you," Betty replies.

"Uh-huh, like David's rock comforted Goliath," Marie says.

They laugh as the maids drive up and begin to unload the things they believe they need to clean the room.

Marie chuckles and says, "I hope they don't think they're here to vacuum and dust."

She gets up from the chair on the porch and walks to the car. "I'm sorry, but this ain't no dust job, ladies. The room has been locked for thirty years and it smells like the rodents that are being evicted as we speak." She looks at the women as they turn to one another.

"The rats will be gone, right?" asks one of the maids.

"Like a fart in the wind," Marie replies.

"We can deal with that. We have lots of ammonia that will take care of the smell," says the maid.

"If the two of you are up to the challenge, I'm willing to pay double what the normal price would be."

The ladies look at one another and shrug their shoulders.

"Show us the room," they say.

"The exterminator is in the room right now. When he's finished, we'll go in and do what we have to do. Now, if you don't mind waiting, it may be a little while."

"We'll wait right here."

Ben is in the room and finds several holes at the base of the walls. It looks like the rats have made several nests in the mattress over the years. Ben calls his brothers and cousins who are back at the office and explains the situation; he says he is going to need their help clearing the room.

When they arrive, he has already exterminated all the spiders, ants, silverfish and other creepy crawlers.

He warns them, "The rats — and I did say rats and not mice — run out through the door or back through the few holes in the walls."

He tells them to carry all the bedding and furniture out of the room and into the backyard. After two hours, the five men have cleared the small room. Ben walks around the house to the front porch and tells Marie what he and his crew have done.

He explains, "The only way we can effectively rid the room and the garage of the rats is to set traps and bait in both places. There are holes at the base of the wall that come from the garage, and they would have to be patched to help keep the rats out of the room if you are ever going to use it again." And then he tells her, "Your husband wants us to leave all that stuff in the backyard. There's a lot of damage to the furniture and the clothes in the drawers, and to the boxes on the closet floor."

Marie signs angrily.

"I'm sorry," he said, "but I'm afraid that nothing in the room can be saved, and the carpet will surely need to be pulled up and replaced too. If you want, I could pull it up for you. The crew and I could have all that up in about an hour or less; that way you'll get most of that foul smell out of the room."

She looks up and pats him on the arm.

"You're doing great. No sense in stopping now."

She then turns to the maids, who have been waiting for an hour to clean the room.

"Ladies, it seems that the men have done all the work."

She gives them double their regular fee and thanks them again for waiting around, and they leave the property. It isn't long before the five men pull the carpet and toss it out into the backyard with the rest of the trash. When they finish, Ben steps out onto the porch of the room and then takes one last look into the gutted space and gives his guys a thumbs-up. He thanks them for their help, and then they all pile up in the truck they arrived in and leave while Ben walks back to the front porch where Marie and her sisters are sitting and making plans for the new room.

"Mrs. Stevens," he calls. "Sorry for interrupting, but we've gutted the room and it's all cleared out. All that stuff is sitting in your yard back there. If you don't mind, I can call someone to haul all that out of here for you!"

She does not even look at him; she just waves her hand.

"Go ahead and do it."

Ben walks back to his truck and calls his friend to let him know that he has a hauling job for him. He gives him the address and tells him that everything is piled up in the backyard next to the garage. He then asks what he is going to charge so that he can tell the owner and get back if the owner agrees. When Ben hangs up the phone, he calls me and tells me everything he did and that he had a friend who will haul all the trash away in a few hours.

I then ask, "Does anyone need to be at the house when he gets there?"

"No, sir," he replies. "Everything is piled up in the backyard. When they get here they will just back up to the trash and load it up on the trailer before hauling it off."

"So what's the damage?" I ask.

"Let me break it down… it will be $450 for the exterminating. We had to set traps in the garage because that's how the rats were getting in. I sprayed for the spiders and other bugs in both the garage and in the room, and then we spread a powder down for the scorpions that were mostly behind all the books and newspapers in the garage. We moved all that from the wall and…"

"Are you still at the house?" I interrupt.

"Yes, sir. I'm still sitting in the driveway."

"Good. I want you to do one more thing — I want you to pull all those magazines and newspapers out and throw it out with the rest of the trash. I knew there were rats because I've seen them run behind the stacks when I walk into the garage."

"Okay, I'll do that when I hang up. Is there anything else?"

"No, please continue."

"Let's see. I was talking about the scorpions... Right, we moved all the newspaper and stuff away from the wall. We didn't put any powder down in the room because I think your wife is planning on cleaning the floor. I charged $450 for removing all the furniture and things from the room, pulling up the carpet, and setting it all in the backyard. The cost for hauling all that off will be $135, $100 for the haul and $35 for the dumping fee. That'll come to $1,035."

"Okay," I say. "Just send the bill to the office and I'll have Janet write you a check. Ben..."

"Yes, sir?"

"Thank you for being so prompt."

"You're welcome, sir. I'll get the newspapers and stuff moved out as soon as I finish here."

"You've been a lifesaver."

"Glad to help, and goodbye."

"Goodbye, Ben."

I hang up the phone and stare out of my office window, worried about what Marie is going through and about the future of my business.

After Ben hangs up, he gets out of the truck to let Marie know that I want him to throw out all the books and newspapers that are piled up in the garage.

"Oh, does he?" she replies.

"Yes, ma'am. Jim told me to toss it all out when I told him that the rats and bugs were using it to nest in."

"Oh. Well, I'm glad you told me that. And what about the room?"

We've cleared everything out of the room, so if you're going to clean the floor you can."

"Will the rats come back?"

"They might, but we set out traps and bait; I'll be back to collect the traps and set new ones. If the traps don't get them, the bait will."

"Well, young man, I can see that you have done a great job here," states Ann. "Let me give you my address. If you think those newspapers and magazines are something, wait until you see my husband's garage. I can't even park in our garage, and I'm ready to get rid of all that old junk myself."

"Here, you can write your address on this form. When I finish cleaning out this garage I'll get my guys together and we'll meet you there and you can show me what you want removed."

"Young man… what's your name?"

"Ben, ma'am."

"Okay. I believe I said remove it all, Ben. This time tomorrow I expect to be able to park that red SUV in my garage. Can you make that possible?" Ann asks.

"Yes, ma'am."

"Alright. Then I believe you have a garage to clean." Ann says.

"Yes, ma'am."

Betty looks at Ann. "Are you trying to hire the man or run him off?"

"Well, I said remove it all, didn't I?" Ann replies.

Marie puts on a brave face. "Ladies, let's go see what the damage is."

They walk around the house to the backyard and see all of Jimmy's furniture and bedding, the clothes he left behind all laid out in the backyard, and his old bike on the porch. With a deep breath they walk into a room that has not been seen by human eyes in almost thirty years, and the smell has indeed subsided a bit since Marie first opened the door. They all just stand inside the room, holding their hands over their noses as they look around.

Betty breaks the silence. "I'll be back," she says, imitating the voice of Arnold Schwarzenegger as she walks off to the house and into the kitchen. She grabs the mop bucket and pours almost half the bottle of Clorox inside, and then fills the rest with hot water. She grabs the broom and the mop and walks back to where Marie and Ann are waiting on her.

Ann grabs the broom. "Well, I'll start sweeping and get all these rat turds out that door, so if you don't want to be hit by a flying turd, get out of my way."

Laughing, they stand at the open window facing the driveway while Ann sweeps the floor vigorously, trying to push her top lip, pressing it under her nose as she tries to filter the stench in the air. When she gets halfway through the room, Marie and Betty run out because they are laughing and covering their mouths and noses with their hands to keep the smell out, or the dust that Ann stirred up. Not long after they've run out of the room, Ann sweeps the rest of the dust and mess outside. Fanning and covering her nose, she blows a large breath out and then walks toward the house, taking in as much fresh air as possible.

Marie calls out to her and asks, "Are you okay?"

"Nothing like rat turds and rat pee-infested dust being sucked into your nostrils like a vacuum cleaner," smirks Ann. "But yes, I'm okay. By the way, if there was a shelf at the top of the closet, I think those men pulled it down."

"Good," says Marie. "There's nothing like reaching over your head blindly sweeping rat poop and probably rat cadavers in your face. Better them than us."

"I know that's right," Betty says with her hands on her hips. Then she asks Ann, "Did you sweep that floor good or just stir up a bunch of dust? I don't want to have a mop full of rat poop when I have to ring it out with my delicate hands."

"Will you get your behind and your delicate hands in there and get that floor mopped?" asks Ann.

"Yes, ma'am," says Betty.

Then she and Marie go in and pour the water and Clorox on the floor, and Betty hands Marie the broom and spreads the water over the floor with the mop. Marie begins to scrub the floor with the broom while Ann watches from the doorway, telling Marie she missed a spot. Not looking back, Marie sweeps some of the water over to Ann, splashing some on her pants. Betty then sweeps more water at the door with the mop; Ann, dodging the water, goes back into the house and finds another bucket in the washroom and fills it with Pine-O-Pine and hot water, and then carries it back and pours it near Betty and Marie, soaking their tennis shoes. They both scream, and then they chase her out of the room with the wet broom and mop. Laughing, they stand back looking at each other and then looking back at the room.

"Time out, girls," says Ann. "We still have a room to clean, okay?"

Looking at each other, they say, "Truce."

"Truce!" Marie and Betty shout while holding the wet mop and broom up at Ann. They all agree to the truce as they had many times before when they were a lot younger, growing up in their parents' house. They walk back into the room and continue to scrub the floor. Ann walks into the garage, where Ben is still working hard to clear the space, and grabs a push broom I use to sweep the walkway. She walks back around to the room and helps scrub the floor. They repeat the process of Clorox and Pine-O-Pine three times. They manage to get most of the smell out of the room and out of their noses too.

Tired, they leave the room, and Marie looks back and sees the holes in the wall just above the floor that joins the room with the garage. She figures with all the stacks of paper and old magazines, and Jimmy's car in the garage, it is hard to notice the rats eating through the wall and destroying Jimmy's room. She remembers asking me to clean the garage out last year when I set out to restore Jimmy's car. Now Marie walks around to the garage and sees a new space — no more piles of old junk where the rats once made themselves at home without a fight. Ben has already left, and Marie cannot be more grateful for his help.

Marie comments, "We can do so much with this room. It's bigger than I remember."

"No," Ann says. "We just got rid of all the things that made it look small."

"Oh, say it ain't so... really, Mrs. Know-It-All," says Betty.

With her hand on her hip, Ann leans toward Betty and sarcastically says, "Seeing is believing, hon."

"Girls, tell me what you think," says Marie.

They look around the room and think how it could be renovated by having a full bath put in by knocking down the wall in the room where the outdoor storage is.

"I think we may have to get rid of that old wall heater, and get a new AC unit with the heater in it like the one Betty has in her beauty salon," says Marie.

"You sure can, sis," says Betty. "So what color will you paint the walls?"

"Not sure yet, but give me a little time and I'll come up with something. I think it's getting late and I have to meet Jim for our appointment."

"None of us is wearing a watch," Ann notes.

"Well, let's go back in the house and freshen up. I can finish cleaning when we return on Monday."

"Return on Monday?" asks Betty.

"Monday," Marie repeats. "Jim doesn't know it yet, but I called and made reservations for us to take a road trip this weekend. I'll fill you girls in and tell you all about it when we get back."

"Wow, listen to you," says Ann.

The three of them walk back to the house and into the kitchen, where Ann and Betty are pushing each other by the sink.

"Girls, there are two sinks," Marie intervenes. "And here the two of you can actually share the faucet... you do see that, right?"

"She must be the middle child," Ann says while pointing at Marie.

"Don't get me started on you, Ann," Marie replies.

"Girl, if I didn't have this gimp in my hip, we'd be rolling like we used to back in the day."

"And who's going to get the two of you old biddies up off the floor while you're rolling in slow motion?" Betty says laughing.

"Oh my god, we used to really go at it when we were younger, didn't we?" Ann remembers, placing one hand on her hip and the other under her lip.

"Do any of you wonder why neither Mom nor Dad would ever intervene?" Marie asks.

Betty interjects, "The real question is… did either of you wonder why I hardly ever got involved? Well?" They just stare at her. "Oh, so you guys aren't going to answer?

"Who are you going to tell now?" says Ann.

"Girl, you would suck up to Momma and Daddy just for a stick of gum," Marie reminds her.

"Should we tell her what we used to call her?" asks Ann.

"You think she can handle it?" asks Marie.

"She can't tell on us anymore."

"Hello, I'm standing right here!" Betty shouts.

Marie and Ann look at each other and nod, and then say, "Bootlicking butt wipe."

"Oh my god, are you kidding me?" Betty whines.

"Girl, you told on us every chance you had. We knew when you ratted us out because you would walk around the house chewing that gum like a heifer chews her cud," Ann explains.

"Okay, now she knows. Here we are, three old ladies who have fought in the trenches over the years for one another, and I love the two of you more than ever." Marie is trying to make up for the old feelings she and Ann had for their youngest sister.

"That is so hurtful. I'm not sure if I like the two of you anymore," Betty whimpers.

Ann grabs Betty and Marie and pulls them close. "We're all we have left," she says. "What we did as kids has nothing to do with what we do for each other now. We are the three best friends in the world — the closest sisters in the whole wide world — and there isn't anything that we wouldn't do for each other."

"Right," says Betty. "I love you too."

Marie goes to the refrigerator and grabs three bottles of water, and she and her sisters walk into the bedroom and talk for a while. Then she shows them the letters that Jimmy sent home, but not the one she left unopened. They laugh and cry, and then Ann and Betty assure her that she made the right decision to go to the room and clean it out. Once they've finished, Marie thanks them for all their help and support.

"I'll see you girls upon my return."

They hug and kiss, and then they leave her so she can get ready for her appointment. After they go home, Marie sits back down at the vanity and cries, wishing I was home and thinking of how much she's missed Jimmy over the years. She takes the unopened letter and puts it back in the box with the others, and then places the box back in the drawer and closes it. She wipes away the tears, gets up, takes a shower, gets dressed, and hurries off to her appointment.

Before she leaves the house, she hears a group of guys in the backyard. She looks out the kitchen window and can see the guys throwing everything on a trailer. She watches as one of the men walks over to the open door of the room and closes it, but leaves the windows open. She walks out of the kitchen with two pieces of luggage she packed the night before, leaving the bags at the door in the living room. She then walks out the front door, locks it, and saunters to her car, which is parked on the street, and then drives off.

61

Chapter 6
The Last Appointment

A big smile shows up on my face when I see Marie driving up to Alice's restaurant. I watch her go through her normal routine when she arrives at her appointment — parking the car, searching her purse for red lipstick, applying too much, and then wiping half of it off. *Late as usual*, I think to myself. At least she waits until she parks to put on her lipstick. I have no clue how some women do that while driving. The routine continues as she checks to make sure her hair is in place, one more check, and I can see her wiping the lipstick from her teeth. The visor goes up, the door opens and a big smile brightens even bigger on my face. I watch her walk across the parking lot and to the door, giving Alice a hug, talking to her, and then following her to the table. I stand to allow her to sit on the bench seat next to me.

"Slide over to the window," she says. "I want you to sit at the window this time because I want Alice to sit here with us. This may be the last time we see her here at the restaurant, and it may be the last time we meet here for our appointments."

"Okay," I say slowly.

"We've been meeting here for our appointments once a month in memory of Jimmy for the last thirty years. This will be one step in the right direction for us to move on and start a new chapter in our lives." She sets her purse between me and the window. "I spoke with Alice after she retired, and then I retired a few months later. Life is too short to allow the past to govern our lives today."

I look up at Alice, who is greeting others as they walk through the door, and then back at Marie.

Marie gives me a quick kiss, and it seems that we both blush for a few seconds. Isabelle walks to the table and brings three glasses of water and two glasses of lemonade before we order anything.

"Your order will be out shortly."

"Thank you," says Marie.

"You're welcome," Isabelle replies, walking away with a smile.

"I know not to ask, so I'll just put this day into your hands," I say.

"Alice told me that it was the right thing to do," Marie explains. "Her grandson has done very well with the restaurant and has plans to do more later on." She turns to me and begs, "Jim, please, let's move on."

"Well, I've been doing a lot of soul searching these past few days," I say, wiping the tears from my eyes. "After your call this morning, it really got me to thinking. So I took a walk and decided to let Brandon take over the company. Next week I'll have to meet with James, our lawyer, and he'll draw up the necessary legal jargon. Then you, James, and I will meet with Brandon after all the paperwork is finished. We'll remain on the board of governors for one year and resign after that. How does that sound?"

Marie holds her hands over her mouth and then puts her arms around me.

"Is this really happening? Jim, I'm so proud of you!" she says.

"Thank you," I reply.

After a few minutes, the waitress brings our food to the table. We bless it and start eating.

"Can you believe it's been thirty years?" Marie asks.

"Believe it or not, our bodies let us know every day," I acknowledge.

Marie stares out the window. "It seems as though time has left a lot of things behind and just moved on. Thank you, Jim," she says with a kiss. "I've been waiting to hear you say that."

Alice walks over to the table and Marie invites her to have a seat with us.

"Jim has decided to announce that he will be retiring," says Marie.

Alice leans over the table, grabs my arm, and says, "Congratulations to the two of you. I am so proud of you, Jim — you are making the right decision."

"Thank you, Alice," I say.

When Alice leans over, we see that she's wearing a locket with an inscription in memory of Drew. Marie comments on how beautiful and ornate it is.

"Oh, thank you," says Alice. "My granddaughters got it for me when I decided to stop carrying my son's letters with me everywhere I went."

"What letters?" Marie asks.

"In all these years I have never told you that our boys were in Vietnam at the same time. My boy Andrew died about a month before your son Jimmy."

Marie gets up from her seat and sits next to Alice. She grabs her hand and asks, "Why didn't you tell us? You were grieving that night you let us in."

"God has a way of bringing people together," Alice says softly.

"But you carried that on your shoulders the whole time you helped us as we went through our grief." Marie wipes the tears from her face. "You should have told us, Alice. We're good friends."

"We all deal with the loss of our children in many different ways, but when you look at it closely, it's all the same. Helping you grieve helped me."

I grab Alice's hands. "I'm so sorry."

"I carried his letters with me every day that I was here," says Alice. "I refused to let them out of my sight. I felt that as long as they were close, I would have a piece of him with me. My husband would tell me over and over to let them go; he told me that I wouldn't move on until I left those letters at home."

"That sounds familiar," Marie says.

"I kept those letters in a plastic bag in my apron pocket. It wasn't until Drew's twins graduated from high school that I took one good look at them and all I saw was my Drew. The spitting image of their father, and it was then I went home and cried and read them again for the first time in over fourteen years. I read one of them where he was telling me that he was going to come home and we were going to travel the country and see the beauty of it all. I remember sending him a letter and telling him I would hold him to his promise. I cried every day I left those letters at home in my drawer. Both of my babies have helped me through it all. It was at that time, when my grandson graduated from college, I decided to let him run the restaurant. It was ten years ago that he came to learn to run the place, and I let him run it a little bit at a time until I knew he could do it himself. Lord knows it wasn't easy at first; he kept telling me he had it, but I just couldn't do it. My heart was still wishing Drew was here."

I stare up at the ceiling and then look down at the table. "I know that all too well." Jim whispers.

"Yes, well, out of all my children, Drew loved cooking the most, so I was sure when he got out of the Army that he would take over and run the restaurant for his mother. I finally got out of the kitchen and eventually out of the restaurant six years ago. We try to go places every three to four months when the girls can take time off work. I did a good job of investing my money. When Drew was talking about doing all that traveling, I knew I had to start saving even though he would never go with us." She starts crying, and so does Marie.

Alice continues, "I saved because I wanted to make his dreams come true, and to keep our promise to each other. It turned out God had a plan for that too. My husband convinced me to invest that money in this newfangled car business, and before we knew it, we had more money than we could spend. My husband Andrew passed away six years ago, so I figured it was time to retire."

"Where in Vietnam did Drew serve?" I ask quietly.

"He was at some camp in the middle of the jungle. He would write me and say that if things got too bad and they had to run, they had an escape route called Route 66," Alice said laughing.

Marie holds her breath, puts her hand over her mouth, and looks right at me. "Isn't that the same camp Jimmy was in?"

"I believe it was… you said he died about a month before Jimmy?"

"Yes," she replies. "On the sixth of November."

"Oh my god! I think Jimmy may have written to us about that day." Marie realizes at this moment that we have both read the letter — the one Jimmy sent to her mother's house.

Unaware that she has read the letter, I turn to my wife and say, "I have a letter at home to show you, and I'm sorry that I never told you of it. Jimmy asked me…"

Marie reaches across the table and puts her finger over my lips. "It's okay," she says. "Don't be sorry."

Alice opens her purse and pulls out a picture of Drew and a band of soldiers in a group. She points at her son.

"This is my son Andrew on the end, holding some kind of gun."

Marie almost screams as she sees Jimmy on the second row with both arms out, but she covers her mouth as she looks at me while I peer down at the picture and point to our son.

"This picture was sent to me in his letter on the second of November in 1970. I don't know why I carry this picture, but I do," Alice says, wiping away her tears. She and Marie continue to hug as they talk more about the boys.

"All these years, and neither of us knew that our sons served in the same unit," Alice says, putting the picture in front of Marie. "Here, child, take a good look."

Marie takes the picture and strokes the image of Jimmy. She then takes a deep breath and wipes her nose.

"If for no other reason, God has brought us together for this very moment in our lives. I too have been holding on to Jimmy by keeping his room sealed like a vault for thirty years. Jim and I are moving on, and this is the day we finally start anew." Marie wipes away her tears.

She looks at the picture and says, "I'll always love you," and then cries before giving the picture back to Alice.

"Today we are going on a little trip after we leave the restaurant," says Marie. "We will be on our way out soon, and go home to drop off my car and get the luggage I left at the front door."

Surprised by this news, I ask, "Where are we going?"

Alice grabs my hand and says, "Just go with it. I know you will enjoy it."

Alice places the picture back in her purse. "I'm also getting ready to go on a trip with my granddaughters. They are on their way here to pick me up; we are going to drive to California to see those big sequoias in Yosemite National Park. It's one of the trips my Drew talked about in his letters."

Then Alice announces that the lunch is on the house. They all hug and bid one another a safe trip and a blessed life.

As they walk to the door, the waitress cleans the table and prepares it for the next customers.

Alice watches the two of them drive off, and then walks to the back and sits in the office, waiting on the girls to get there. She looks up at the pictures on the wall of the office. Some of the old pictures that used to hang on the walls of the cafeteria have been removed and replaced with new pictures that reflect

the new look of the restaurant. She turns around in her chair and picks through some of the pictures that were packed away in a box on the floor, wondering if she should take them home or leave them here in the restaurant.

Chapter 7
Red Beans and Rice with Corn Bread

November 5, 1970

"*H*ey Sarge, they're serving yellow bricks and calling it cornbread again," says Stevens. "You're the third cat who told me that. I was just about to go over there and mix that fool up a batch. I gave him the world's best cornbread recipe and he is still serving bricks."

"Yeah, take a look at this." Corporal Stevens takes the cornbread and bangs it on the edge of his tray.

"Ohhh!" shout Sergeant Williams and the other brothers in the company as they reel back with their fists up to their mouths.

"Hell no!" Private Jones complains. "I ain't eating that rock. You have to soak that brick overnight just to cut it with a fork. Come on, Sarge. You have to go over there right now and fix that man some real cornbread. Go over there and show that fool what real cornbread is."

"Damn! I could take that and press it into bullets and use it when we run out of ammo," says one of the privates.

"Man Stevens, don't eat that. If it don't break your teeth out, it'll give you the squirts. I don't know what he put in that, but I know I ain't eating it." Private Jones turns and gives Goodtime some dap before he walks away.

"Stevens, you should throw that shit in the can where it belongs," says Goodtime.

"I hear that," Sergeant Ramos says.

"Yo, Stevens" calls Sergeant Williams. He then speaks quietly, holding his hand on the side of his face. "If you can wait, I have some of my mama's red beans and rice cooking up in our bunker, and some cornbread too. Toss whatever you've got in the trash and come by the bunker in an hour. And you keep that to yourself."

"Sarge, what are you doing?" shouts Private Brown.

"Back up, Private. This soldier is from my hometown."

"Yeah, but I bet he ain't from the same side of the tracks," Corporal Mann says with his fist muffling his mouth.

"Don't pay any of them fools no attention. They trying to keep it all to themselves, and they can't eat it all, so be there in an hour."

"Got it, Sarge. Thanks!"

After an evening of eating good food that Williams cooked in his bunker, most of the men are hard asleep. Corporals Stevens and Wayne step out into the dark and see Sergeant Williams and a few others outside their bunker talking in one of the holes made by a mortar a few days back.

"Two peas in a pod. What's up this too-quiet night?" Sergeant Williams greets them. They sit in the hole with the guys.

"Not much, Sarge. To be honest, I like it quiet."

"All this time and you boys ain't learned to read the quietness," says Williams. "This is one of those nights the VC could be crawling across that killing field, cutting their way through the wire so they end up right next to you. And you wouldn't know it until they put that bayonet in your chest."

Gunter puts his hand to his chest. "Yeah, I don't think I want to go that way."

"Me either," one of the guys says. "Just shoot me and get it over with."

"Like hell," Williams says. "Give me my ticket out of here and send me back to Hawaii."

"That's what I'm talking about," says Private Baptiste. "Man, I got a girl waiting on me when I get back to the island."

"Yeah right, this fool gets his first kiss and now he thinks he's in love," Private Jones teases.

"What time you have, Sarge?" asks Private Jones.

"About midnight," Williams replies.

"Yeah, I guess I'll turn in and get some beauty sleep," says Jones.

"Hell, you going to need more than one night to do that, boy!" Private Mann tells him.

"That's funny coming from somebody with a face like a baboon's ass," says Jones.

"Knock it off," Williams orders.

Wayne and Stevens thank Williams for dinner and leave to go back to their bunker for the night.

The night is quiet and a little cool, the sky is clear, and all the stars are brightly shining. Two o'clock in the morning, and all hell breaks loose when mortar rounds hit one of the tents set up on one side of the camp and other targets selected by the enemy. Everyone who is still in the hole jumps out and runs to a foxhole, while others are yelling, "Incoming!" Men are popping out of the bunkers like ants with their rifles at the ready, engaging in a fire fight with an unseen enemy that is firing mortars and AK-47s from the woods.

Williams called out to Corporal Wayne.

"Get that fifty-cal hot!" Williams shouts. "And get a move on!"

Williams runs to a foxhole and fires his M-16 at shadows in the dark. Flares are fired to illuminate the open field and tree line; a couple thousand VC can be seen running. He fires until his clip is empty, reloading as he continues to fire at the shadows.

A mortar round hits the front of the foxhole where Corporal Gunter Wayne is firing the fitty. It goes silent for a few seconds, and then it picks up again. Another mortar hits the foxhole, and it's silent when Corporal Wayne is blown out. Wayne moans and Williams calls for a medic to assist him. Knowing they need the fitty, Williams crawls to Wayne and pulls him away from the hole when the medic lets him know Corporal Gunter Wayne is already dead. Williams rolls over into the hole and checks the fitty before climbing out and running to another foxhole where Private Mann is shouting at the enemy. Williams sets up the fitty and begins firing, and notices that some of the VC are getting through the wire. He fires at the wire cutting down as many as he can with the fitty. Then more of them hit the wire and someone hits the foo gas and the night explodes into a fiery ball. Men are screaming that they are caught when the barrels of thickened fuel explode. Sergeant Williams stops to reload the fifty-cal when two VC run past Williams's foxhole and into one of the others to shoot Private Daily.

"Keep firing!" Williams orders Private Mann, but he does not respond. Williams looks down and Mann is lying on the ground; he's been shot in the head. Williams starts firing the fitty again when a VC runs up from behind him, firing his AK-47 into the foxhole and shooting him in the back several times.

F-4s and A-1 Skyraiders begin dropping napalm, rockets, and five hundred pounders on the treeline and the clearing. After a couple of hours, the night is as quiet as it was before it all started. Everybody stays in their holes until day begins to dawn in the valley. When they know that it is safe, they begin to clear the perimeter while the choppers patrol the tree line and surrounding area.

Sergeant Williams and Private Mann are pulled out of the foxhole, and their bodies are placed in a tent to be shipped out. Corporal Connors, one of the cooks, walks in and gives his last respects to Sergeant Williams. He pulls from his pocket the recipe that Williams wrote for Sergeant Whitley.

"I promise you that for as long as I live, I'll make cornbread the way you meant it to be, and if you don't mind, Sarge, every once in a while I'll start cooking some of those red beans and rice with this cornbread recipe."

He pulls out a flask, unscrews the cap, and takes a swig. "For you, Sarge," he says, and then salutes, turns, and walks out of the tent.

Chapter 8
The Home Comings

*E*arlier sitting at the table, Alice holds Marie's hand. "I knew God would work things out if you allowed him to."

"I'm glad you prayed for us that first night we met, but I'm still upset because you never told us about your son," says Marie.

"Alice," I call, getting her attention, "you know so much about us. Tell us how you got this restaurant started."

"Yes!" says Marie, patting Alice's hand. "We've all been so busy that we have never sat down to really get to know each other."

"My word!" Alice says, closing her eyes and thinking back to over sixty years earlier.

"I started working in my parents' restaurant sweeping the floors when I was six years old. My father started the restaurant in 1932, just a few of blocks from the church he pastored. At that time, it was no more than a shack, which helped feed the hungry during the Depression before the United States got involved in World War II in 1941. Those were hard times back then. Food was scarce, but my mother made sure we had clean clothes. She checked that our hair was combed, and we stayed prayerful every day."

I laugh and add, "Those times were really hard. I wore the same clothes every day, and they didn't get washed but maybe once a week."

"My mother was much like yours," says Marie. "We didn't have much, but we had to keep our clothes washed and our hair combed. I guess you could say we had to keep up proper appearances."

Alice grins and says, "That or get the strap."

We all laugh together.

She continues, "There were twelve of us, seven girls and five boys. At least nine of us were doing something in the restaurant. I was often referred to as Number Eight by my older sisters and brothers." Alice reminisces about her childhood days. "When my oldest brother Willie Jr. wanted something, he would call out, 'Hey, Number Eight,' but I wouldn't answer him because I was not a number, so I would tell him that my mother gave me a name. He called David 'Lucky' because he was the seventh child. He had a nickname for all of us. It got to the point where only our parents called us by the names they blessed us with. DK2 was what he called the twins, because Maggie and Millie were always duking it out with somebody. When they weren't arguing with each other they were fighting, and when they weren't fighting they were getting whippings."

Marie laughs. "Sounds like my sister and me."

"Well, those two were always getting into something. In those days the boys' job was to keep the restaurant repaired, and to keep the old stove that one of the members of the church donated to us working. Back then it was really hard work but Daddy was not one for excuses. If he told you to do something, you did it, no questions asked.

"After the Japanese bombed Pearl Harbor, three of my older brothers left for the war. My three oldest brothers volunteered, Willie Jr. and Abraham in Navy, While Isaac (Number Four) joined the Marines. Willie Jr. and Abraham served in the Pacific, and Isaac served in Guam. In those days, Daddy listened to the radio all day, every day, and when he wasn't listening to the radio he was reading the newspapers. If you wanted to know anything about the war, you could always go to him, as many in the church and neighborhood often did. At home, there were many days my sisters and brothers would leave the house because we could not change the radio station."

Lowering her voice and leaning forward, Alice adds, "We often went to our friends' houses and listened to music on their radios. Daddy kept his radio on the news of the war all day with very little music in between," she remembers.

"The only time we sat around the radio as a family was when one of his favorite radio shows was on the air. Amos and Andy, and Jack Benny was our favorite.

"I remember those shows," says Marie. "They were wonderful."

"Bud Abbott and Lou Costello, we can go on and on," I interject.

"That's right. So we listened to all those shows. Sometimes I think listening to the radio is better than watching TV as we do today, since you can use your imagination," Alice replies.

"Well, today I can't get anything done before I watch the soaps," says Marie.

Alice continues, "Honey, I find myself doing the same thing." They laugh. "Most of my older brothers and sisters grew tired of working at the shack; it was long hours and no pay. That was the real reason behind the three oldest boys volunteering for military duty. Two of my oldest sisters wanted to join the military too, somehow, someway, but Daddy would not have it. Josie, Number Three, and Jean, Number Five, found out that the Army was accepting women in the military. That was all they needed to know, and by December of 1942, they took the first bus out and joined the Women's Army Auxiliary Corps. Near the end of the war in 1945, they were assigned to the 6888th Central Postal Directory Battalion."

Marie and I listen intently without saying a word.

"Daddy would stand in the pulpit and talk about his children who were serving in the military. He would pray for all our men and women who were serving their country in that war. Daddy often fussed about the girls being in the Army, but he was proud enough to preach about them being among the first black women to serve overseas. After the war, all of my sisters and brothers came home, but their stay was brief. Willy Jr. left for California, and Isaac married a woman he met in Philadelphia and moved to her home state. Josie saved up her money from the Army and moved to Canada, while Jean married and moved back to Florida, where her Army career had begun. She took a job at the post office there, using her experience from the Army. Among all of those who came back, Abraham stayed the longest. He was a cook in the Navy, so he helped with the restaurant for a year until he fell in love. He and his wife followed Willy Jr. to San Diego, California.

"I had been there working in Daddy's restaurant for a long time, and in all the years, I have seen my brothers and sisters leave because no one wanted to work there. I knew how they felt because I felt the same way."

"Is that where you met your husband Andrew?" asks Marie.

With a big smile on her face, Alice says, "Andrew was a transplant from Tennessee. He moved to Texas, moved in with his sister Deborah who was a member of our church." In a dream state, she adds, "When I first laid eyes on him he looked lost in the church. I tried small talk and found he had not long gotten out of the Army. He was six feet tall, well-built, and what impressed me the most was he was well-mannered. Daddy wasn't impressed because he felt he was taking another one of his daughters from the restaurant. It turned out he was right. In 1947 I turned twenty-one, quit the restaurant, married Andrew Williams, and moved to San Diego, California in Logan Heights at Willy Jr.'s request. It wasn't hard to find a job at a restaurant. My experience was a big help, while Andrew was trying to get work at the harbor. The money I made was the only money we had coming in at the time. It felt good to get paid for my work; after all, with the work and hours I put in at Daddy's restaurant, there was never a penny given. Daddy demanded long hours and hard work, and even our lunch was taken while we worked. Many a time we would leave a hot plate of food, only to come back to a cold plate. When we left for California, I said I would never return to the restaurant."

"Sounds like my brother," I add. "When he left home, he said he would never come back."

"Did he?" asks Alice.

"No. He moved to Wyoming after he retired from the Air Force and never looked back."

"Why did he leave so angry?" She wondered.

"Oh, he and my father just didn't see eye to eye. That's all I know — I was sixteen when he left, and no one ever wanted to talk about it."

"We all have our reasons," says Alice. "When I was in California, I received letters from Mama regularly. She said that only four of my siblings were left to help in the restaurant, and she was getting a little worried. If the last one left, they would have to close the restaurant. I couldn't help but feel sorry for them, but I just couldn't be coaxed into coming back. Most of the time I was too tired to write home, and I would only go to my room, jump in bed, and go to sleep. When I was pregnant I worked until a week before the baby was born. Those were hard times for the two of us, but we made it through. All of our children were born in California, but Mama's letters kept coming in and I did all I could to resist the pleas of going back.

"In 1960 Drew was going on thirteen, and I had been working with Abraham in his restaurant for five years. That was when I got a letter from Mama saying that Daddy had a heart attack and could no longer work in the restaurant. So I thought it would be a great time to take over the place. With Andrew's help and support, along with Willy Jr. and Abraham's encouragement, I told my brothers and their families' goodbye and moved back here to Texas. I celebrated my thirty-fourth birthday trying to hold on to the old shack. I convinced Millie and Maggie to help while Andrew and Drew and a few men who my family helped a few years back came to renovate the old place. They completely rebuilt the restaurant with a proper kitchen and a small dining room. We spent all the money we saved over the years, and it was time we opened the doors to our customers. The main meal on the menu was our grandmother's old recipe for red beans and rice and sweet cornbread with a piece of chicken and collard greens. Jobs were scarce, so we could not overprice our plates.

"So we sat down with Daddy and Mama and talked about adding seasonal dinners and lunches to our menu. It was something we did in California at Abraham's restaurant. A bowl of red beans and rice, our gumbo soups, and chicken and rice soups would go for 25¢, and the meal for $1.50. Our Thanksgiving and Christmas dinner for $2.00 came with turkey, giblet gravy, sage dressing, collard greens, and sweet potato yams. Together Millie and Maggie made a killer sweet potato pie and pecan pie we sold for 10¢ a slice."

I sit back in my seat and say, "Wow, now that's a menu. Those were the days. Sounds like we should be coming here for Thanksgiving. Makes my mouth water just listening. Now I'm going to have some of that pecan pie you've got back there."

"Make that two slices," adds Marie.

Alice gets the attention of one of the waitresses.

"Could you bring two slices of pecan pie, please?"

"Yes, ma'am."

"Thank you, baby."

She walks away to get the pie.

"Now where was I?"

"That mouthwatering menu," I say with a smile.

"Right. Mama's garden supplied most of the vegetables we needed, and we would get our meats from Mr. Williams's farm. He was one of the church members. We tried to keep our costs as low as possible by buying from the church members. We made Daddy proud by the way we ran the restaurant. I guess by then he was as impressed with Andrew as I was, and in his own way he forgave him for taking me to California for thirteen years. He loved the children, and especially Drew, who took to the kitchen like a master chef. If it came through the doors he wanted to cook it; he was a natural. In 1964 Daddy had another heart attack and passed away, and it was the first time since the war that all my sisters and brothers were together under one roof. Mama was so happy we were all together again, even if was only for a couple of days.

"Drew was a good kid. In high school, his girlfriend LeAnn got pregnant with twin girls, Amanda and Alice. Drew and LeAnn were married in June, and in late October the twins were born. We all talked about how he could stay on at the restaurant, and as time passed he would get raises. He would see better pay later, but Drew believed that he could provide for his family better if he joined the Army. After enlisting, his entry date was set for November 1965. I was so happy that he got to see those two precious little girls before he left for boot camp.

"Drew, LeAnn, and the twins lived with us in the house my daddy bought. We lived in the house that Daddy renovated from a duplex he had purchased to house fourteen people. He tore down some of the walls and converted a kitchen, living room, and dining room into bedrooms, so there was more than enough room for all nine of us.

"After Drew left for the Army, he sent more than half of his checks home. Most of it, he sent to LeAnn and the girls. LeAnn and I sent Andrew letters at least three times a week. I wanted to always keep in touch with my baby. The money Drew sent really helped — we added a new stove in the kitchen and more tables and chairs in the cafeteria. Whenever Drew had leave time, he would come home and really spoil the girls. The last time he came home was in 1967, right before he left for this place called Vietnam. None of us even knew where this Vietnam was. When he got there, he would write us as often as he could and we would do the same.

"I knew how I felt whenever I got letters from Mama, so I did not bother him too much about the restaurant. Besides, the war was keeping him plenty busy. LeAnn continued to work in the restaurant and I found out that she was a pretty good cook. When Drew was cooking in the kitchen, she was always by his side. When he left for the Army, she filled in and the two of us were just sweating up a storm. Of course we had a bigger storm going on with Millie and Maggie always raising sand in the kitchen. Those days they just did it to get on each other's nerves, not to mention everybody else's."

They all laugh.

"How long did they work here?" I ask.

"Oh, Maggie's husband retired in 1981, and she retired with him. Millie stayed on for another five years, but because of her health, she had to retire not long after," Alice replies.

"Did LeAnn stay on?" asks Marie.

"No," says Alice as she looks at Marie. "LeAnn remarried in '76 and started working at the post office. My sister Jean called LeAnn and told her that she should check to see if the post office was hiring in our area; LeAnn already had a friend working there, and it turned out they were hiring. She went down and took the test and not long after that they hired her on. Now, I was short a cook, and for the first time I understood why Mama was worried about having to close the restaurant because everyone was moving on in life. It was foolish of me to think that I could hold on to my family just because I paid them. All the same, I was proud of LeAnn for getting a job she could retire from. She and the girls moved out after she married and lived across town, so I was still able to see my grandbabies whenever I wanted. My oldest daughter Elaine was married and living in South Houston and had three children. Lynn was married and living in Berkeley, California with her husband and three children, and David was one of the Associate Ministers in the church and was engaged to Barbara Evers, whose family were longstanding members of the church. 1987 was the first time we hired outside the family. There were enough young people in the church looking for work, so we started hiring them; of course many of them only stayed for a short while. No different than today, I guess."

"You're right!" I exclaim. "We tried hiring young kids ourselves, some of them got their checks on Friday and didn't bother coming in on Monday."

"And they don't bother calling either," says Alice.

"No, you're just short for the day," notes Marie.

They all enjoy themselves on this last appointment. They laugh, they cry, and they comfort and reassure one another that they will keep in touch. The day goes well, they exchange hugs and kisses, and then they say their goodbyes.

Chapter 9
Just a Letter Away

*I*t feels like a full day to Alice after sitting down for the first time in a long while to have lunch with Marie and me. We talk to one another, and then Alice slips back into her office, closes the door, sits in her chair, closes her eyes, and thinks back almost thirty years ago to the night Marie and I showed up after she locked the door in January of 1971. She had taken a little time off from the restaurant because on November 8, 1970 she received a visit from a Casualty Notification Officer and the chaplain. It was Sunday morning, and she and her mother Helen were getting Amanda and Alice, Drew's twins, ready for church. The chaplain knocked on the screen door, and Mama Helen greeted him on the porch.

"Good morning, ma'am, we are looking for Mrs. Williams," he stated.

"I'm their mother," she said, talking to the two men through the screen door. "Who exactly are you looking for?" She turned back to look at Alice and LeAnn, and then softly met the gaze of the two men.

"We're looking for the wife of Sergeant Andrew Williams, ma'am," the Casualty Notification Officer replied.

Andrew walked to the door to see the two men and knew right away why they were there. He reached for the screen door handle while taking in a deep breath. As Alice walked up to the door with her hands to her mouth, and with LeAnn not far behind, he grabbed her by the shoulders. Alice immediately felt dizzy and nearly collapsed on the floor. Andrew asked Mama Helen to open the screen door and let them in while he walked Alice to the chair next to the front window. Elaine and Lynn helped LeAnn to the couch on the other side of the room. LeAnn and Alice refused to accept the letter, so Mama Helen took it instead. In the midst of all the crying, she told them, "They're not listening right now," and then wiped the tears from her own eyes and wept.

Alice screamed, "No, no, no!" loud and long as she fell from the seat to the floor, kneeling down as she grieved for her son. "My baby, my baby."

Andrew had dreaded this moment; he was eight years older than Alice and knew all about the soldiers' visits. He had served in WWII, and although he wanted his son to come home when the war was over, he knew in the back of his mind that this day might come, and that he would have to accept it. Drew's letters were all too familiar to Andrew; they were no different from the letters he and his fellow soldiers had written home.

And for many, the letters were the only things that made it home. Being a truck driver in France as part of Patton's Red Ball Express, he saw many bodies on side of the road and in the open fields, and thanked God that he was alive and able to come home to his family. Now he stood listening to the chaplain express his condolences, and Andrew could only listen while trying to hold back his tears. He shook the men's hands and thanked them for the personal notification, and then let them out, closed and locked the door, and took Alice to bed.

He asked Mama Helen for the letter that was left behind and read it. He wiped the tears from his eyes, but could no longer hold back and began to sob as he fell across the foot of the bed. After a few minutes, he composed himself and walked into the front room. He had everyone sit down so he could read the letter to them. LeAnn took the girls and cried for most of the day; she did not get out of bed for three days. No one went to church that Sunday. Mama Helen made a call to the church and informed everybody of his passing. All week they were visited by friends and family. Andrew drove to the restaurant and placed a letter on the door to let everyone know the restaurant would be closed. It was two weeks before Alice returned to the restaurant with all the letters Drew had sent to her that year in her apron pockets, while LeAnn stayed at home for another week contemplating what was best for her and the twins.

She talked to her family, looking for the encouragement she needed to move on and go back to work. Late that night, she, Alice, and Mama Helen talked about Drew and the decision she needed to make. After three weeks, she returned to work. The night Jim and Marie showed up at the restaurant, Alice had only just walked to the door and locked it no more than five minutes before they pulled on the knob. Alice, LeAnn, her daughters, Lynn and Elaine, and her sisters were cleaning the restaurant after a long day. Her husband Andrew and her youngest son David were in the back cleaning the grill and stove as her two brothers-in-law watched and talked. Earlier she had placed Drew's letters in her apron pocket, along with the Western

Union letter notifying LeAnn of her husband's death during his third tour in Vietnam. Alice went into the restroom to read the letters; afterwards walking to the front of the restaurant to help clean, although she stopped when she heard someone at the door. At the door she found a tired couple who appeared to be hungry. Her father never let anyone leave hungry, even if it meant opening up a table after closing to send them away with full stomachs. Alice called out to them as they walked away.

"Hello there."

They turned around and apologized, wishing they had gotten there earlier.

"Nonsense," she told them. "You look tired and hungry. All I have left is a little bit of red beans and rice and some cornbread. You folks are more than welcome to have that if you like."

When they entered the restaurant she sat them down at one of the tables near the window in the middle of the cafeteria. She brought them a plate of red beans and rice and a saucer of cornbread with tall glasses of water. As she cleaned, she noticed the woman wiping away tears that seemed to flow as she looked out the window. It seemed as though she was expecting someone to join them.

"They must be pretty hungry," Maggie said. "They have had two helpings."

"Shush," Alice said. "Let them be."

When they were finished eating, they wanted to pay.

"This is on the house," Alice said. "The next time you folks visit you can pay."

She walked them to the door and let them out as they continued to protest the free meal. Alice looked at Marie as she spoke to her.

"I couldn't help noticing you crying at the table. Is everything alright?"

"We lost our son in Vietnam, and this is the first time we've been out in six weeks," Marie replied.

Alice felt a sickness come over her. She put her hands in her apron pockets, clutching her letters from Drew.

"Well, you look like good Christian people. Would you mind if we pray?" Alice asked.

She prayed for them in the cold night air, and when she finished, she assured them that she knew God would help them through it all. As they walked away, she said, "Good night, and be careful on your way home."

When she walked back into the restaurant, Maggie and Millie met her at the door. The men stood at the table closest to the door waiting on her to speak.

"Okay, Number Eight, you want to fill us in?" Maggie asked.

"Well, I noticed she was crying and I asked what was wrong." Alice paused as she clutched the letters in her apron pockets.

"Okay," Millie said with her hands out. She then dropped them to her side.

"She told me that their son was killed in Vietnam, and that this is the first time they have been out in six weeks. So I prayed for them."

Leo and Floyd looked at Alice and Andrew with sympathy, shaking their heads and then quietly gesturing to their wives that it was time to go.

"Well, we're still praying for you," said Maggie. "You do know that, right?"

"Yes, and I love you all for it," said Alice. She reached out and grabbed the two of them, giving them a big hug and kissing them both on the cheek. She closed the restaurant that night praying that they would be alright.

As Alice continued to wait for Amanda and Alice to pick her up from the restaurant, she looked around the old office and thought, *I never wanted to force my children to work in the restaurant, but they helped out all the time and as much as they could. They all stayed until they were married and then moved on with their families to start off on their own life's journey. I have been so blessed for so many years.*

Opening her purse, she pulls out the picture she showed to Jim and Marie, takes a deep breath, closes her eyes, and remembers her husband Andrew's attempts to get her to leave the letters home.

October 3, 1970

Hello Mother,

I know I promised I would be home for Christmas, but it seems that things have gotten as hot here as they are when Aunt Maggie and Aunt Millie are in the kitchen together, and that's pretty hot. I kind of miss all that — Dad, Uncle Leo, and Uncle Floyd acting like they're trying to stop them but only after egging them on a little and then stepping back to watch. LeAnn tells me that things haven't changed a bit there. These are the times I wish I was back in Hawaii, only this time with my family. It's really warm here and some of the guys ain't used to this kind of heat; some of them are from the north where it's cold half the year. Being a Texas boy we're used to this. Sure wish I had some of your cooking because ain't nothing anybody can do to make this slop taste like food. I tell all these clowns they ain't had no food until they ate some of your red beans and rice and a heaping side of cornbread, a big piece of chicken and some mustard greens. Every once in a while I get the chance to cook up a mess of beans and rice and some old-fashioned cornbread. These fools around here almost fight just to have some, and when I invite others outside of our gang, they get all upset about it. Good thing I have the rank because I invite them anyway. Your last letter said they shipped old Henry back to Texas after he lost one of his legs. You tell him to take care of himself. I'm going to start calling him Hop-Along Henry from now on. Kiss the girls for me.

Love you,
Drew

October 12, 1970

Hello Mom:
I got your letter. Tell Pops I hope he's feeling better. Thank you for taking care of my three girls; I'm really digging the pictures you sent of them. The twins are really growing up. I hope they are not giving you too much trouble. I miss them a whole lot these days. I write LeAnn at least twice a week when I can. The noise the twins make all day around the house ain't

nothing compared to the noise the NVA makes around here. The girls used to get on my nerves with all that screaming and banging on stuff; I don't see how you do it, but I guess it's like Aunt Maggie always says, that "the best time is rest time." I sure would be glad to trade right about now.

I wish I had some good news. They sent us out last week to take some hill (don't know why, we just turned around and gave it back to them) and while we were being dropped in by the choppers we only got about half a klick in the bush when we were ambushed. It was like they knew that we were coming or something. Three days of fighting and I tell you there ain't nothing like hearing bullets buzzing by your ear. You're busy trying to keep your butt down so you don't get your fool head shot off. I don't rightly know how many of our guys are dead but I was show-nuff happy to kiss the ground after the chopper landed back at base camp. I was glad to get back and kiss the girls' pictures. I wish I had a real plate of food right now — this ham and lima beans is the worst, we call it ham-n-chockers. Well I'm a whole lot of tired right now, so I'll send this letter off so I can get some sleep. Kiss the girls for me.

Missing you all,
Drew

October 30, 1970

Hello Everybody,
By now, the girls are looking forward to Halloween. Funny thing here, I really don't have much to say. There's this cat that let me borrow his cassette player yesterday. I thought I could record most of my day and send it to you and the girls. I was reading this magazine and I saw some of the most beautiful places back in the world. When I leave this rock, we are going to travel around the country and take in some of the sights, the waterfalls, the mountains and all the trees. Did you know that they had what they call a sequoia tree in California that cars drove through? It fell down last year. I sure don't remember nothing like that when we lived in San Diego. Can you imagine what that must have been like to have something like that fall? I want to take you guys there so we can see those giant trees. I want you and Dad to travel with me, LeAnn, and the girls. I want us to see the world. When we are in the choppers flying over the trees, it's just as beautiful here as it is there. It's hard to see the beauty from the ground when you have your head down, but it's a sight to see when you're in the air. We're going to do some traveling when I get home and see all the beauty of our country. I can't wait to see you. Anyway, kiss the girls for me.

Love you,
Drew

November 2, 1970

Hello Mom and Dad,

I hope this letter finds the two of you in good spirits. I know that you are praying for us here because the NVA thought it to be a good time to test our defense here at base camp. We knew something was wrong when everything was just too quiet, and then around two in the morning, all hell broke loose. This wasn't one of their harassment tactics. They came right up to the perimeter and we fought them for about thirty minutes and then it went silent again just like it was before it all started. This hit and run thing can run a man crazy. We lost about eight men in that fight and now we are on high alert. I heard that our base was not the only one they hit this morning. There were two others. I can only thank God I have praying parents because I hear this is getting as bad as it did back in '68. It's not helping any with them politicians reducing the number of troops because that just means we have a lot less men to shoot back at the enemy. Those NVA ain't no joke — they know when our numbers are smaller and they take advantage of that. I tell you these are some scary times here on this rock. Kiss the girls for me.

Miss you and love you,
Drew

EST Nov 8 70
GOVERNMENT PD WASHINGTON DC

MRS. LEANN WILLIAMS
105A N. AVE E STREET
WARM RIVER, TEXAS

THE SECRETARY OF THE ARMY ASKED ME TO EXPRESS HIS DEEP REGRET THAT YOUR SON, SERGEANT ANDREW WILLIAMS II, DIED IN VIETNAM ON 6 NOVEMBER 1970, FROM WOUNDS RECEIVED WHILE IN COMBAT OPERATIONS WHEN HIT BY HOSTLE SMALL ARMS FIRE. PLEASE ACCEPT MY CONDOLENCES.

When Alice finished reading, Andrew walked over to the table and hugged and kissed her. He asked, "Do you want me to fix you a cup of coffee?"

"And have the whole house sitting at the table with us sipping coffee all night? No, I don't think so."

"Okay," he said.

She got up from the table and kissed him while picking up the letters from the table.

"Thank you anyway," she said, turning to him. "Wipe that funny grin off your face; I have a headache."

They laughed and went to bed for the night.

"Alice," Andrew whispered. "You have to learn to let go and move on, and if you don't you're sure to go through some kind of depression and make it hard for those around you."

"Andrew, we've talked about this before."

"Yes, I know. We all miss him and wish he was still alive; but he's gone and there ain't nothing we can do about it. We have three beautiful children who are hurting just like the rest of us, and two beautiful five-year-old grandchildren who depend on us."

Alice sighed and rolled over.

"Please go to sleep, Andrew."

"I love you with all my heart and I will always be there for you." He says. "So I'm asking you — begging you — to please do your best to leave those letters here at home. I know at the restaurant every time you go to the restroom you're reading those letters, and when you walk back through the kitchen holding your head down I can see you've been crying."

"Please, Andrew."

Alice just rested in bed with her back to her husband, not wanting to say a word. She waited for him to get tired of talking about it, roll over on his side, and go to sleep.

"Baby, we have to start living for ourselves. What do you want me to do? I want to help."

"Then go to sleep and don't bother me right now."

Andrew sighed and rolled over, hoping she could talk to him about it.

"I won't read them anymore if that will help."

"It's a start, baby girl. I love you."

"I love you too."

For the next month she stopped reading the letters, but she still carried them in her apron pockets. To keep them from getting dirty she wrapped them in cellophane, although she still took them to work with her every day. After six months, she began saving money so that they could travel the country just as Drew had planned before he died. After more than eight years of saving, Alice had nearly $9,000.

One Saturday morning, Andrew walked into the kitchen reading the newspaper with a bunch of wild ideas about how to increase their savings by investing. He wanted to take their hard-earned savings and invest them in some companies that were near bankrupt ten years prior and were now making a comeback.

"Andrew, listen to me. You ain't saved a dime of that money and I ain't about to let you lose it all on some bankrupt companies."

"Alice, these companies ain't bankrupt; I said in the early seventies they were near bankrupt."

"Walter…"

Andrew sat up in his chair, looking at Alice over the top of his glasses.

"You got something you want to tell me, woman, calling me Walter? Who's this Walter?" he asked.

"Yeah, I called you Walter because that's who you're sounding like right about now."

"And I ask you again, who is Walter, woman?"

"Walter's that fool in that play… *A Raisin in the Sun*. You remember he went out with every penny his mother had and lost it on pure foolishness, stupidness, whatever you want to call it. He came back broke and had nothing to show for it."

"Alice, let me invest just half that money, and if I lose it I'll pay you back every penny."

She laughed out loud. "Empty your pockets, Andrew."

"What?"

"You heard me. Empty your pockets."

He reached into all his pockets and pulled them inside out.

"Just as I thought. Broke as a hobo."

"Come on, baby."

"Oh, it's 'baby' now. What happened to 'woman'?"

"Alice, you're being unreasonable."

"I liked it better when you called me 'woman'."

"Alice."

"Andrew."

They sat at the table staring at each other until the twins came into the kitchen.

She greeted them as they walked to the stove and looked into the pot of grits.

"Good morning, girls."

"Good morning, Grammie."

"Girls, come here a minute!" Andrew called as he turned to them for support.

"Nope. We're not getting into that discussion. Sorry, PowPow."

"Smart girls," Alice said.

Andrew got up from the table and walked back into the bedroom.

"You think we were too hard on PowPow?" Amanda asked.

"No, baby, he's going to sit on the toilet for about thirty minutes and come back in here with another one of his plans."

They laughed and then told her, "You know we looked into the companies PowPow wants you to invest in, and they look pretty solid. Chrysler named their new chairman, Mr. Lee Iacocca, and there's a lot of changes going on in that company. Just last year, they appointed him as the president of the company, and in one year, he's chairman. I think you have to act fast while the stock prices are at their lowest."

"Yes, but..."

"Grammie," the twins interjected, "it's a sound investment."

"Well, we had better get ready to go to the restaurant, and be ready to open by eleven o'clock, okay?" Alice asked.

"Okay," they replied.

"You know you don't have to help at the restaurant today. It's your Saturday to be off, you know, and you might want go to the movies or something."

"No, we're good."

"You girls finish eating and don't tell that grandpappy of yours we had this talk."

They laughed and said, "Okay."

It wasn't until Alice talked to her granddaughters that she decided to allow Andrew to invest $4,500 of the money she had saved. In 1979, she handed the cash to a smiling Andrew, who promised she had made the right decision.

"I don't believe in all this," Alice said. "But you see that rolling pin over there?"

He looked cautiously over to the sink where it sat.

"Lose my money and I'm going to use it on you."

"Baby, I'm..."

"Don't 'baby' me; do what you said you're going to do, and you'd better do it today because if you don't, I'm going to change my mind."

That morning he called Vanguard, a company that one of his customers told him he could trust. The customer also said the price of the stock may be over one dollar and ninety cents a share so Andrew would have to buy it at the asking price of two dollars a share. Without hesitating, he purchased a couple thousand shares before going to the restaurant that Friday morning. When he arrived at work, everyone was waiting on him.

"Well, Walter," Maggie said. "Did you do it, or do we get to hold you down and give Alice the rolling pin?"

Looking at the family and their faces, he decided to abandon the notion of a joke and just show her the account information. He told them, "This is a long-term investment and we should not look to super returns overnight."

"What do you mean 'long-term'?" asked Alice.

"Five, ten years tops. We can sell at any time."

Alice sank in her seat and put both hands over her face.

Millie told Maggie to go and get the rolling pin while she held him down.

"You people ain't making this easy. Let me talk to my wife. Once she understands she can tell you."

"Humph," Maggie and Millie said as they stormed off to the kitchen. Andrew walked over to the table where Alice was sitting.

"Baby, I purchased two thousand shares at a cost of two dollars a share. I deposited $4,500 so we still have room as it rises and falls for the next five to ten years. Stocks rise and fall in a single day and over the next few years it'll do the same. Honest, Alice, it's a good investment. They say that the stock can rise as much as ten dollars or more. That has the potential to more than quadruple our investment. I'll show you the newspaper every day so that you can help me keep an eye on it."

"You'd better not turn into a Walter, you hear me?"

"Loud and clear, baby girl."

"You won't be hearing so loud and clear if you lose my money. You'll be as dizzy as a mule-kicked man when that rolling pin gets to you."

"I see I'm going to have to hide me a rolling pin."

"Do what you have to do, but I'm expecting good things in five to ten years."

It wasn't until January of 1987 that Alice wanted to sell the stock. In both accounts the money had grown to more than six figures over eight years, and she wanted out with no questions asked.

"I'm nearing sixty-one years old, and I'm not getting any younger. Besides, I took our remaining savings and let Amanda and Alice invest it with some of their own money. They invested it in that same company you chose. We sold it all in December of last year. The government wants their share of the money, and it was time for the IRS and I to share that investment. Andrew sold our shares and paid all the fees, and we talked to an accountant to figure out what the taxes would be on that money.

"I gave you that money because I love you," she explained. "But I knew that it was the girls who talked you into investing it before you came to me. They came to me with their wild ideas in '79, and then you came to me with the same wild ideas not more than a month later. I just want you to know that."

And then she gave Andrew $10,000 to do what he wanted to do with it.

It wasn't until Amanda and Alice graduated from college in 1988 that she decided to leave the letters at home. They purchased a gold ornate locket for her that she still wears today. The inscription reads, *In memory of Andrew Williams II,* and it has a picture of Drew inside.

Alice's Andrew died in 1994 at the age of seventy-six, and he was buried in the same memorial grounds as Drew for his service in the Army from 1941 to 1945. In 1995, on Alice's sixty-ninth birthday, she decided to retire and turn the restaurant over to Anthony, her grandson.

Chapter 10
Promises to Keep

Marie and I leave the restaurant, and I follow her home so she can park her car. She sees that all of Jimmy's things have been packed away as she pulls into the driveway. As I exit my car, I watch my wife close her eyes and take a deep breath; she turns the engine off, opens the door, and slowly gets out. I walk over to her and give her a big hug. With the curtains removed from the windows, I can see the empty guestroom, and the cleaned-out garage. I walk Marie to the front door and open it, and there I find the luggage at the door.

She asks me to help take the luggage to the car for our weekend getaway in Canton, Texas. She walks across the living room, picks up the phone, and calls Janet.

I take my time walking out the door trying to listen to her phone conversation.

Janet answers the phone. "J. Stevens, this is Janet. How may I help you?"

"Hello Janet, this is Marie,"

"Mrs. Stevens, hello! How are you?"

"I'm fine. How are you?"

"Great! Is everything okay?'

"Everything is wonderful; I've never felt better. The reason I'm calling is because Jim is taking some time off and won't be in next week. He'll call after that and we'll be in for a special meeting the following week."

"Okay, I'll inform Brandon and the others."

"You do that and enjoy your weekend."

"Thanks! I hope you do the same."

"We will. Goodbye."

"Goodbye!"

She hangs up as I walk back into the room. Marie tells me about the conversation she's just had with Janet.

"I told Janet you will be taking some time off. That you will not be back next week."

"Okay, and where are we going?" I ask.

"I booked us a little cabin in Canton just off the lake. It'll be just the thing we need to relax and get away."

"Well, I'm ready to go."

"And so am I."

I open the door for her and walk out behind her so I can lock the front door.

Overwhelmed with excitement, she kisses me before we walk off the porch and make our way to the car.

"We're going to be okay," she says.

We climb into the car and let the roof down. I back out of the driveway and we begin our new adventure.

She wraps a red and white polka-dotted scarf over her hair and puts on her sunglasses.

"What kind of music do we start off with for our trip?" I ask.

Marie shuffles through the stack of 8-track tapes and selects The Bee Gees. As we travel down the road, we listen to "How Can You Mend a Broken Heart."

She raises her hands in the air, and I smile as we cruise down the road.

Alice's granddaughters arrive at the restaurant thirty minutes after Marie and I leave. Before they arrive, Alice walks to her grandson's office, which used to be a large storage room. Before sitting down, she gives him a big hug and a kiss.

"I am so proud of you and everything you've done for the restaurant."

"Thanks, Grammie."

"I won't ask you to keep any promises; when I took over the restaurant, I did things my way and now I expect you to do the same."

"You don't have to ask," says Anthony. "I'm just building on all the great things you've done over the years. You've invested your life in this place, and I will do the same."

"You have a good head on your shoulders, and I surely hope you keep it that way."

"If I don't, that wife of mine will remind me. And if that don't work, she'll tell me about a rolling pin that I have no recollection of its whereabouts."

She laughs as she remembers threatening Andrew with the same rolling pin.

"Boy, if nothing else lasts around here, that rolling pin had better. It's been around for as long as I can remember. You'd better not throw it away — it belonged to my mother."

"Grammie, you know how much I love you. Did you say you were taking it home with you?"

She popped Anthony on the back of the head. "Alright boy, you best behave yourself and Laura won't have to use it on you."

"Grammie, there's a box in your office with all the pictures you said you wanted. I'll drop it off at your house after work, okay?"

"Uh huh," she says slowly, giving him a kiss on the cheek before walking out of the office for the last time.

"You enjoy your trip, Grammie, and don't forget to bring back lots of souvenirs for your favorite grandson."

She laughs. "Bye, favorite grandson."

After she leaves Anthony's office, she walks around the restaurant. Then she approaches the table where she, Marie, and I were sitting for lunch. She looks out the window, remembering that fateful night we met some thirty years ago.

Alice smiles softly.

Looking out the window, she can see Amanda and Alice pulling up into the parking lot. She turns to walk up to the front door and out to the entrance, and climbs into the backseat of Amanda's BMW X5, opens her purse, pulls out a Mahalia Jackson CD, and then asks Amanda to put it in for her.

Amanda inserts it into the CD player, and they listen to the song "You'll Never Walk Alone" as they head up the highway, north on 27 before connecting to Highway 40 going west.

Before Alice left the restaurant, she watched the wait staff walk the customers to their tables. The waitress came by the booth where she, Marie, and I had sat, and noticed a photo of a group of Army soldiers in Vietnam lying on the table. Looking at the photo briefly, she turned around and walked back to the front, well aware that Marie and I had been there with Alice earlier.

More books by J. Lew

Novel
The Witches and Wizards of Ozz – *Deep Impact*
Rock, Paper, Scissors – *Reflections of Life*

On the Table
Sepulcher – *The Devils Den*
The Witches and Wizards of Ozz – *Kingdoms Divided*

Children's books
A Chris Adventure book Series

I'm Not Afraid of The Dark
Sunken Treasures

Soon to be released
Little Ranch Hands
Chris's Family Vacation at Rocket World

We would like to hear from you
____

Visit our website at:
www.jlew-books.com

www.ingramcontent.com/pod-product-compliance
Lightning Source LLC
Chambersburg PA
CBHW051709180726
48283CB00004B/1267

9 781946 806161